ALL MEASURES NECESSARY

BY

STEVEN KAY

All Measures Necessary

Copyright © Steven Kay 2017

The moral rights of the author have been asserted.

Cover © Steven R Kay 2017, 1889books

Cover Fonts: "Misproject" and "Nailscratch" Courtesy of
Eduardo Recife © Eduardo Recife/Misprinted Type
[http://www.misprintedtype.com]

www.1889books.co.uk

ISBN: 978-0-9935762-5-6

Author's Note

I wrote this in 2016 – the calling of a snap election in 2017 rather spoilt my planning. Rather than waiting for a raft of further rejections from conservative, risk-averse publishers and literary agents, or trying to re-write it given fast-moving political events, I decided to publish and be damned.

This is a work of fiction. None of the people in it are real: everything is made up from that disturbing place that is the inside of my head. If you think you recognise characters – that is in your head, not mine. There is no autobiographical element to it whatsoever. The clue's is in the name: fiction.

If by chance you enjoy reading it, or even think it is any good it would be great if you could write a review on Amazon or Goodreads or whichever online sites you use: just a line or two would be great. Perhaps even recommend it to your friends. Word of mouth is so important when you've not got a marketing department and financial backing behind you. Thanks.

Every operator must take all measures necessary to prevent major accidents and to limit their consequences for human health and the environment
— Control of Major Accident Hazards Regulations 2015

We declare our right on this earth...to be a human being, to be respected as a human being, to be given the rights of a human being in this society, on this earth, in this day, which we intend to bring into existence by any means necessary
— Malcolm X

I t all started with the dog in the window. A Jack Russell. Nothing
unusual in that. I was told it often sat there – waiting for its
owner to return. Sometimes it slept on an old blanket on the
window ledge. What was unusual was that the dog didn't appear to
have moved all day. It was there when the neighbour went for his
morning paper and was still there in the afternoon when he came
back from his lunchtime pint at the club and his trip to the bookies.
The dog was imaginatively called Russ. His owner, David Pitts, was
a postman so his return from his round often fitted in with the
routine of the neighbour returning from his leisure pursuits.

The neighbour would often look out for Russ, who sat watching
every movement for Dave's return – steaming up the window with
his breath and pink, floppy tongue. The neighbour said he
sometimes used to wag his walking stick and bare his false teeth at
the dog to wind it up, but that day there was no such fun to be had.

He didn't want to be seen to be nosey so it wasn't until the next
day when he saw the dog still in the same spot that he thought he
perhaps ought to check "the little fella." He pushed open the gate,
something that would normally set Russ off, and went up to the
window. The dog's tongue was hanging out of his mouth and he
was still. The neighbour tapped on the window but Russ didn't
move. He rang the bell, which was a sure-fire way to get the stupid
thing yapping, but the Westminster chimes were the only sound
from within. He peered in through the letterbox – nothing but a
waft of warm foetid air emanating from the slot. The police were
called and broke in via the back door.

It was two days after, late in the afternoon, that I got a call from
a PC Shaw that set events in chain. Just as I was thinking of ending
my day's battle with visit reports, and wondering whether to buy
stuff to cook or to succumb to the all too usual takeaway. My boss
wasn't in – off furthering her career doing important things at the
bidding of senior civil servants as usual.

'There's been a death at Canklow – the incident number is 15 of
Tuesday: a carbon monoxide poisoning it seems. The name of the
deceased was David Potts, or Pitts, aged 42. The DCI wondered if

you might have an interest, since the boiler appears to have been recently installed.'

'So… what… you think there could be a defective installation?'

'That's a possibility. So, we'd like input from the HSE.'

'And this was, what, two days ago?'

'Yes, we found the body at around 2 p.m.'

'And what are you wanting from me?'

'The inspector has requested attendance from the HSE. How soon can you get there? He said he'll meet you on site.'

Typical bloody plods. Expecting you to drop everything and come rushing – like you are some sort of service to assist them, on call twenty-four hours a day. No problem. Just pop the blue light on the bonnet: be round in a tick. They do their usual: of assuming they know everything, before it occurs to them, as an afterthought two days later, that there could be wider factors.

There was no time to get support from a specialist gas engineer that day. Another evening screwed for no reward.

It was well-gone six o'clock and dark outside when I arrived at Canklow, after my battle with Derek Dooley Way and the Parkway. It was obvious which house it was from the squad car and forensic vehicle outside.

'Mitchell Miller,' I said, showing my warrant. He didn't offer me his hand.

'Inspector Drake. Watch your step,' he said. 'There's crap everywhere – not quite literally, but almost.'

I kicked my way past unopened post and miscellaneous items of clothing in the hallway. The house was cold – doors and windows had been opened: clearly to try to reduce the smell. It was apparent that the occupant wasn't the most house-proud of individuals. The kitchen was a mess: empty tins of dog food and old, foil containers from curries, pots piled in the sink, and a floor as sticky as a fibreglass bath factory.

As Inspector Drake spoke I started scribbling notes in my notebook.

'The deceased was found upstairs in the bathroom – he was wearing just his underpants and had vomited. At first we just thought he'd been drinking, there's plenty of evidence of that, as you can see. But the scenes of crimes boys pointed out his pinkish tinge might suggest carbon dioxide poisoning.'

'Carbon monoxide.'

'Yeah. Anyway, we found receipts for the boiler – it was only put in two months ago.'

I smiled at a young woman in a white paper coverall coming downstairs with a pile of plastic evidence bags; she stepped gingerly across the rubbish-strewn hallway.

The inspector nodded towards the SOCO. 'We're still going through his papers – needless to say it's not filed alphabetically.'

'Any P.M. results yet?'

'No.'

'Had he been dead long?'

'A day or two. It was a neighbour who alerted us.' He flicked through his pocketbook: '…a Mr Scrimshaw of number thirty-two.'

'And what other appliances are there?'

'A gas fire in the front room, I think.'

'And next door? Have they been questioned?'

'Of course, but they didn't have much to do with the deceased. There are no suspicious circumstances.'

'But have they got gas appliances?' The Inspector was clearly confused. 'Well we'll need to rule out the possibility of migration of carbon monoxide from next door. Have they been told to get their appliances checked?'

'No, I don't believe so. That hardly seems necessary.'

'Well, if you want to rule out the possibility of further deaths. It is quite feasible that there isn't always an airtight barrier between terraced houses – crumbling mortar, poor construction, that kind of thing.'

He raised his eyebrows. Somehow, I didn't believe it was his decision to call in the HSE. Probably the forensic scientist had mentioned it and that meant he had to tick a box.

'I'll go and speak to them, unless…'

'No, leave it with me. I'll get one of my PCs to go round.'

'They need to look out for yellow flames on gas fires… and ask them about when they got their appliances serviced last.'

He got on his radio and went out of ear-shot.

The front room didn't look like it was used much, except by the dog who was also assumed to have died from carbon monoxide poisoning. There would be a post-mortem on the dog as well.

The wall behind the boiler in the kitchen was unfinished – in need of plastering where the brickwork was exposed, but I couldn't see that Mr Pitts would have been too concerned about a patch of brickwork given the state of the rest of the room. I took down what make and model numbers I could without removing the cover and cleared a space on the worktop to climb up to look at the boiler more closely. So, maybe not the best practice for a safety inspector to use a chair to step up onto a worktop, I know: Work at Heights Regulations and all that shit, but I carried out a dynamic risk assessment – okay? A question of do as I say, not as I do.

The interesting thing was the flue pipe – it didn't appear to be terminated into the boiler properly from what I could see – it was hard to tell visually from my awkward position on the worktop and I didn't want to touch anything.

The inspector came back through into the kitchen.

I looked up from my note taking. 'I suggest you get the Scenes of Crimes Examiner to photograph this flue connection. This is a possible source of our leak. Has anyone been up here or moved anything?'

'No, I don't think so. I'll check.'

I got down off the worktop.

'What I would suggest is that, as soon as I can in the morning, I'll get our engineer to come and run a test on the boiler.'

'I've been making enquiries about bringing in our own gas engineer – someone who will be able to provide us with expert evidence. We have to be careful to preserve the evidence chain. It has to be done according to CPIA.'

He spoke like he expected me to ask what CPIA was. Patronising sod.

'That's what our engineer does. We are not strangers to this. I was about to explain…'

'But the engineer will need to be recognised by the courts as an expert witness. I have procedures to follow. I am dealing with a potential homicide here, not just an industrial accident.'

It shows you just what a professional I am that I didn't just roll my eyes but looked him straight in his. 'You will not find a more *expert* expert. Our engineer has years of experience of investigating gas incidents. Did you have someone better in mind?'

'Er, I need to make some enquiries.'

'Look, is this to be a joint investigation? Do you want to follow the protocol for investigation of work-related deaths or shall I just leave it all to you?'

He was not pleased with me. His face said it all, but I didn't care. I was tired and had had enough of being treated like a lackey. I had been here several times before: playing second fiddle to coppers.

'So, what we'll need to do is run the boiler for several hours with the house empty – what can happen, you see, is that after a while the boiler gets starved of oxygen if it fails to draw in enough fresh air from outside, and then you get a spiralling of incomplete combustion. We'll need to get the neighbours to vacate their properties while we run the test, so that there is no risk of anyone else being affected.'

'I might need to bring someone to oversee this test.'

'Bring who you like but we should take advice from HSE's engineer.'

'We're definitely looking at a defective installation then?'

'It seems likely. We can run basic checks on the neighbours' appliances at the same time. But we'd best advise them not to use them for now.'

I checked in the back yard where the flue came through the wall – treading carefully to avoid the dog mess in the dark. The flue wasn't very well finished from what I could see by torchlight, there was a gap around the bricks where it went through the wall, so the flue was not fixed very well.

The Inspector was waiting in the hall ready to get off to more important things. I reported my thoughts on the flue.

'Do you think we can get fingerprints done on this flue pipe after we have done the test tomorrow? That way we can verify who it was that fitted it? Might it be sensible to get a PCSO posted, so that other possible key-holders don't come in and disturb things before

morning? Especially if the positioning of the flue pipe is crucial'
Twice as much as me this guy was probably getting paid.

The local newspapers were full of the story – it was the dead dog
that attracted all the sympathy – not the middle aged balding bloke
found on his bathroom floor in dirty pants, covered in vomit. Even
back at the office it was: "oh, the poor dog!" No thought for poor
Dave and his loves, his life, his contribution to the world. Such
hypocrites! Poor dog! Never poor calf when they tuck into the plate
of veal or poor chicken when they buy their cheap, southern fried
chicken – the product of the cruellest factory farming. You
shouldn't eat the stuff if you can't face how it was made and how
the animals suffer at the end. That's one thing about this job: you
get to see it all – the factory farms, the slaughterhouses and the
terrified animals waiting their turn, the squealing pigs as they are
stunned and jerk about as they are hung up and stuck, to be drained
of their blood. Not that I'm judgmental, mind.

We ran tests the next day – stood around outside in the cold
while the inside got warmer and warmer. Every three minutes we
checked the readings coming off the monitors tracking the carbon
monoxide levels, but we couldn't find anything conclusive – these
things never follow the script. The boiler was managing to suck
sufficient fresh air in through its flue to avoid vitiation – the
spiralling of incomplete combustion – despite the poor termination.
Once we'd cleared enough space to get a decent stepladder in, we
could see that there was indeed a gap where the flue had come free
from the elbow joint. The engineer's opinion was that the weather
conditions could make all the difference – just a bit of breeze in the
right direction being enough to change the flue's balance. We
thought back over the previous few days of cold, still air – those
days where radio newsreaders get muddled with their "fost and
frog."
The gas fitter who had recently installed the boiler was arrested
and bailed. I was not consulted over their discussions nor invited to
join in the interview. Typical of the police – there's nothing they can

ever learn about investigation, the words "subtle" or "considered" not featuring in their official-issue dictionary.

They find it hard to believe that someone such as me could even be a Tier 3 interviewer – like interviewing skills was their sole preserve. So much for it being a joint investigation. So much for our lead on gas safety legislation. In the end the CPS dropped the case without any reference to HSE. They didn't think there was sufficient evidence for manslaughter charges. The mess of paperwork was handed to us. My boss asked for a report and I spent hours trying to weigh up the evidence. The interview with the gas fitter was full of gaps – the police hadn't considered all the technical angles – but to go back and interview him would have been a waste of effort after so much time had passed. And he had had months to rehearse all his arguments at the inquest and in court, and been coached by his solicitor. The file didn't even have details of whether the flue pipe had been fingerprinted to determine who had touched it. I checked with the police and just got an email back saying I'd been given everything there was. We had the flue pipe in an evidence bag and I suggested getting it fingerprinted ourselves, but my boss rejected the idea – with a swish of her highlighted hair and a wave of a lacquered nail – as neither merited nor a good use of public funds on such a vague hunch.

I still recommended prosecuting him for not being a registered installer – that was the best I could do – but even that was rejected – a technical offence not in the public interest – since the incident he had completed his registration and satisfied the assessors of his competence. Someone dies – and a "poor wee innocent dog" dies – we move on. More targets to hit – more fees to harvest to spare the Chancellor of the Exchequer's blushes.

I thought little more of it – other worries and concerns came along every day to knock the last ones, squawking, off their perches. Life's triumph of the immediate over the important.

TWO

Christmas and New Year's hangovers came and went, the suicide and relationship breakdown season, Saturday coach trips away to Walsall and Colchester, shivering and getting soaked to the skin in the salubrious surroundings that a Tuesday night's match in Rochdale presented.

But there's something to be said for routine to get you through those days when you forget there is a sun in the sky. Work broken up by the pub and gym, the never ending excitement of watching eleven journeymen knock lumps off your team in a game that has nil – nil written all over it, only to end in defeat from a last minute set piece, the occasional fumble up a blouse in a taxi home from town and Sunday lunch with my mother up at Owler Bar. I even took her on a day trip to Harrogate at Easter and treated her to scones and jam that set me back more than a South Stand ticket for a Category A game. But then I am a dutiful son.

The papers had been branding it as a "winter of discontent," – in reality no more than a "winter of mild and polite grumbling," in a very British, early twenty-first century kind of way. But it was not going away. Instead it was turning into a spring of slightly more vexatious agitating, with the distinct prospect of it building to a summer of apologetic revolution.

It had started with that vanguard of the working classes – the junior doctors. Years of a failed philosophy of austerity were causing greater strain on the NHS. Somebody somewhere was lying and the public were starting to realise that perhaps the government's claims to be pumping more and more money in were a bit suspect. The junior doctors were sick of being blamed for failures of policy and cranked up the pressure.

It had spread everywhere: there'd even been unrest in the armed forces as the cuts in the MOD affected logistics and backup for the frontline soldiers who were also dying as a result of disasters worse than the Nimrod scandal. Government energy policy, or the lack of it, had led to occasional power cuts. And all of this was combined with an economy deep in recession again following the collapse in the pound and a political elite that had made a hash of trade negotiations.

Others in the public sector had also started getting awkward. It was one thing when we saw our pensions and salaries being slashed, but now people were starting to die as a result of not getting treatment or decent home care, or from being thrown out of their homes. They might as well go round shooting old folks and the unemployed – that's what my cousin Pete, who works in Social Services said – the outcome's the same, only cheaper.

Everything we had been saying was coming to pass, and the public were coming on to our side at last. Suicides were being reported: caused by depression and mental illness inflicted by trying, but failing, to keep vital services going, despite working flat out.

A few weeks before we had had a one-day strike across the public sector: and unlike David Cameron's "damp squib" back in November 2011, this one was pretty solid: we were catching the curl of a wave of public opinion this time. How brilliant it was to be marching up High Street alongside doctors with stethoscopes round their necks, fire-fighters, librarians, contracted-out bin-men and care-workers, and council staff. And what really got me was people – ordinary people – stopping to applaud. Years of Tory mismanagement and incompetence surely fizzling out?

I called into the office first thing one day to collect my kit bag for a day's inspecting in the badlands between Rotherham and Barnsley. A constant drizzle kept the windscreen wipers busy smearing the glass and had me pledging yet again to get new wiper blades. The first visit of the day was an engineering works which machined components for the offshore industry. I had just parked up on the main road of the industrial estate when, out of the corner of my eye, I caught sight of a figure approaching me crossing the road.

'Mr Miller. I'm really sorry to have to do this, but I followed you from your office. I couldn't risk phoning you.'

The man was in his early thirties, jeans and a reefer jacket, with a Unite Against Fascism badge on the lapel. I felt for my phone in my pocket and looked to see which way to run.

'No, please don't. I'm nothing to worry about – I just need to speak to you about Dave Pitts.'

It took a second for me too fish the name out of my memory.

'Why, what about him?'

'Not here – can I buy you a coffee? Then I'll explain. There's the garden centre just up the road with a cafe. I'll follow you there.'

My mind was racing the whole of the two-minute drive – I considered trying to lose him or driving to the police station, but I was curious, and he didn't seem threatening. In fact my gut feeling suggested he was a decent sort of bloke.

He parked next to me near the entrance.

'Thanks. I appreciate this. I wouldn't be doing it if it wasn't important.'

He ordered a pot of tea for me and a coffee for himself and we sat down in a corner away from the retired baby-boomers, resting after their stresses over colour co-ordinating their bedding plants, slurping their lattés – coffee for those who've never been weaned off milk: sweet hot milkshake for overgrown toddlers who still crave their mummies to tuck them in at night. Never trust a man who drinks latté.

'My name's Josh.'

'I'm Mitch.'

'I know, and I know I can trust you. I need some help – your help. Dave was a mate of ours – he was a good man – a CWU steward for nearly twenty years – only ever thinking of others. We don't believe his death was an accident.'

'Hang on, who is *we*?'

'I can't tell you that. Let's say we are all union people – believers in democracy. We think Dave was deliberately targeted and taken out.'

'Oh, come off it.'

His whole demeanour told me this was no wind up. I sat back in my seat.

'I know you investigated. How likely do you think that is? I mean, could it have been deliberate? The *Advertiser* and the *Star* didn't give much away – they were more interested in Dave's dog than him. It just doesn't make sense.'

'What am I getting involved in here? You're not MI5 or something?'

He smiled. 'No, nothing like that – just on the same side as you; same side as all decent people.'

'And which side is that?'

'This isn't a game. I know you're politically on the left. I know you hate this Government and what they are doing. I know you're a vegan, that you live in Woodseats, that you support Amnesty and dislike multi-national corporations and their contempt for democracy, that you've been on recent TUC rallies, like what is happening in the Labour Party…'

'Hang on, how…'

'Don't pretend to be surprised, Mitch. It doesn't take the CIA to work all that out – you only need to spend two minutes on Facebook and Twitter to work out a profile down to your inside-bloody-leg measurement. I bet we could even have a good shout at your passwords. We also know that you were an NUS officer at UEA, and active in the Green Socialist Alliance up until the 2010 election.'

'I had to give that up – I have to be non-political in this job. I am not allowed to actively canvas for any politician or party any more. Besides, it was going nowhere – that. Maybe if Philpott gets in we'll get a fair electoral system – it's rigged for the Tories.'

'It will take something close to a revolution to change it, but that might not be so far off the way things are heading.'

'No chance. The best we can hope for is a bit more fairness, a bit more redistribution of wealth. The government might change but the rest is subtle shifts. People in this country are far too complacent – too wrapped up in their own lives.'

'Like you've become? Mitch Miller, average guy, living out the remaining forty years of his allotted three score and ten, waiting for someone else to do something.'

'Hang on, that's not fair! I don't need this shit.' I got up to go. 'I'm up for a fight when the time comes. I do what I can, but life's too short to waste in committees and talking shops. Passing resolutions and amendments… it's like the People's Front of Judea.'

Josh leant back in his seat and smiled. 'I thought it was the Judean People's Front?'

'Splitters!'

Grey heads turned as the two interlopers lowered the tone of the garden centre cafe by laughing out loud. I sat back down.

'Go on then. You've got my attention, but it was months ago. Why you so bothered now?'

'It's just some things we're picking up from what's going on; from the word on the street. It's starting to get serious.'

'What is?'

'Never mind; tell me what killed Dave.'

'But why can't you just put in a Freedom of Information request?'

'And you think that would tell us what we need to know? Jesus wept! Mitch, this is important – there's something very nasty going on against people like you and me.'

'But, assuming I do talk to you, what would you do with that information. I've got my job to think about.'

'Nothing to drop you in it, if that's what you're worried about.'

'Thanks for the tea, Josh. Let me have a think. If you know me as well as you claim, you'll know I'm a cautious man – not easily led.'

If truth be known I was inclined to fob him off: like chuggers who come to your door or collar you in the street. "I'm just very busy, give me a leaflet and I'll consider it carefully," kind of thing.

'Come on, Mitch – all we need is a bit of help.'

'But say I do tell you stuff. If it came out: it's not just a sackable offence – Official Secrets Act and all that – but inspectors can be imprisoned for disclosing information. With great power comes great responsibility.'

'Voltaire?'

'Spiderman.'

B ut I struggled to ignore what Josh had said. It was like an earworm – a snatch of *Bad Romance* that some idiot plays in the pub.

The thought of a murder kept bubbling back to the front of my mind as I clocked up the kilometres on the machines at the gym that evening – "starting to get serious" he'd said. I thought back to the boiler – it was entirely possible if a little fanciful. But then, since I had been doing investigations of gas work, I had often reflected how easy poisoning with carbon monoxide would be as a way of getting rid of someone. If you think about it everyone's boiler flue sticks out from the wall. Just bunging it up wouldn't do the job because most, these days, are sealed so they don't draw air in from the building, but if you could work it loose and break that seal or crack the plastic by hammering a rod through the vent…? And gas fires? They are open to the room and most people don't bother with carbon monoxide alarms. Or even – what if you could get hold of a carbon monoxide gas cylinder and pump it through an air-brick under someone's floor in the night? Would the plod even do more than think: must have been something wrong with their gas fire or their grill, then they went to bed and died in their sleep.

Houses are so well draught-proofed these days that just leaving your grill on can be enough to turn all the oxygen in your room into carbon monoxide. It happened to an old couple, I remember, who wanted to cook a joint for Sunday dinner but their oven burner didn't work so they use the grill burner instead – they nodded off, Songs of Praise and Countryfile came and went, but they never woke up.

And carbon monoxide displaces the oxygen from your haemoglobin so readily. Would the police even bother to check carbon monoxide cylinder sales from Alibaba.com? It's nasty stuff carbon monoxide – not called the "silent killer" for nothing – like a snake it can creep under the floors, even up walls from the flat below and in through your open bedroom window at night. Worse ways to go I suppose, though.

I showered at the gym and changed. It was dark when I parked up outside the pizza place on Chessie Road. I was definitely unnerved thinking how much information was out there on me after what Josh had said – I looked around for people watching me, but the street was quiet.

I love this pizza place – it's not just the usual stuff – they put interesting stuff on to make up for the absence of cheese: chillis, asparagus, artichokes and decent olives. And they sell cheap bottles of wine too, for people like me who can't be arsed to go two doors down to the offie. And you can get a boxed salad to assuage any sense of fast-food guilt.

I balanced the pizza and salad on top of my sports bag, Italian plonk in the other hand, kicked the car door shut, and made my way up the passage. I dropped the bag outside the back door, unlocked it and flicked on the light switch. I put the pizza box and bottle on the table. A large figure appeared at the open door. Black beanie hat, unshaven, dark-skinned.

'Don't forget your bag,' he said smiling.

'What the…'

'Don't panic, Mitch.' Someone else spoke from behind the big bloke. It was Josh stepping into my kitchen.

'Get out. I'm knackered and want my tea.'

'Don't let us stop you. This is Abdi by the way. He's a rude bastard – no manners.' Abdi had a big grin on his face. Josh sat himself down at my kitchen table. 'Put the kettle on Abdi, eh?'

'For fuck's sake! Can't you leave me alone.'

'We're not doing this for fun. Me and Abdi have got better things to be doing this evening too.'

Abdi still had his beanie hat on and had taken two mugs off the mug tree. He waved one at me.

'No thanks, I've got this.' I took the bottle over to where the cupboards were and got out a glass. 'Coffee and sugar in that cupboard there. There's no milk.'

'Any chance of a biscuit?'

'Tin – on the side, there.'

I got out a plate and cutlery then put them back deciding to eat the pizza straight from the box with my fingers, just keeping a fork for the salad. I wasn't going to put on any airs and graces, or treat these uninvited guests as friends. They could have the instant coffee in the jar, reserved for washing-machine repairmen and the likes, rather than the decent stuff in the freezer.

'We've come to persuade you one way or another.'

'Another?'

'There's no option really. But we're nice people. Perhaps you don't realise just how serious this is. It is a matter of life and death for us – quite literally. We're not playing games here. There are forces stacked against us that would rather see us dead than see us succeed.'

'You're not making any sense,' I said through a mouthful of pizza.

Abdi sat down with two mugs of black coffee: my Cuba Solidarity one, and my favourite Lane Legends one that my Dad had bought me. I never let anyone else use that one – it was sentimental; he pushed it towards Josh with none of the reverence it demanded. Josh inspected it and approved, which eased my anxiety. At least he wasn't a Wendy.[1]

Abdi was not far off my age, I guessed, perhaps in his late twenties, a bit jowly, stockily-built, thick black stubble that must be a nightmare to shave and nice eyes: dark, chocolatey, with long lashes – I like that in people. Thin lashes always make people look a bit lizard-like.

It was Josh who replied. 'We've got the Tories rattled, what with the election not far off – them and their mates – the ones you never hear of any more – not since *Searchlight* disappeared – or was strangled.'

'I still don't get what you're on about.'

'The editor didn't die of a heart attack, as was the official line.'

'No? What do you mean?'

'We believe he was taken out. The replacement, *Stop Racism*, is toothless and a puppet of the establishment – anti-racist Prozac.'

Abdi sat nodding.

---

[1] A mildly pejorative term for a Sheffield Wednesday fan.

'This is just conspiracy-theory nonsense. What's it got to do with me?'

Abdi spoke: 'Not nonsense. Dave Pitts was a mate, see. A comrade. We had to take most of our work underground, build networks, use word of mouth and union brothers and sisters to build strength – get out on the door steps and talk to people direct, use social media because the BBC has been totally fucked by the ruling classes. All these new members we've got since Philpott got elected – that's the way to win this. Dave was a top bloke, he had built a massive membership and was a bloody good organiser – people looked up to him and he could put things into the right words and enthuse people for the cause. He was a massive loss, and not the only one. We need to know what happened. If we're to be able to react.'

'React?'

Josh stepped in: 'The people we're up against will stop at nothing to keep Labour out of power. Tell us what you know of Dave's death.'

Abdi was watching me closely with his big eyes looking over the top of Che Guevara as he blew steam off the mug.

I took a long swig of the cheap red, which didn't taste so bad now after that first glass, and started on the salad from the plastic container.

I wiped a smear from the glass. 'There was something a bit odd about it, if I'm honest. The flue wasn't secured into the top of the boiler and it seems that that, combined with the weather, meant the combustion air wasn't coming from outside but from inside the house. But it was a relatively new boiler so it was put down to a defective installation. There was deemed to be insufficient proof against the installer. He said it was sound when he installed it and says that the flue in position wasn't the one he installed and he had some paperwork which seemed to back that up so it was dropped – no charges.'

'So what was odd about it?'

'Well that flue pipe, and the fact it wasn't the right one, and the police didn't do a very good job of investigating – they didn't take prints off the flue pipe.'

'So, could it have been interfered with? Is that what you're saying? And could that be done from outside the house?'

I nodded. 'It looked like foam-sealant had been used around the hole through the wall at some stage – not a great idea, but it had been removed and the new flue pipe was quite loose in the wall.'

'Where's this pipe now, has it been destroyed?'

'I think it's still in the evidence room at the office. I noticed it in there the other day and meant to tell someone to get rid of it.'

'It would be interesting to see if there are any prints on it,' Josh said turning to Abdi. 'We could then compare it to the database?'

'You have a database? Exactly who are *you*?'

'We've told you – friends. But we're not just bumbling amateurs – there is a war on and we need to be serious if we're going to have any chance of winning it. The stakes are incredibly high. We need to match those against us as far as we can, strength for strength, even though we don't have their billions to draw on and a huge state machine to tap into. Can you get us that pipe?'

'I should imagine. I'll just stay back late one evening when most people have gone home.'

I immediately regretted opening my mouth. I should have kept a clearer head, not drunk anything. But the wine had loosened my tongue and brought out my rare sociability. That, combined with a bit of pride at being picked out and recognised for my worth: something that was very rare in my line of work, where performance was managed not by rewarding success but by dropping like a ton of shite on anyone who failed to meet performance targets for whatever reason, be it, rarely, incompetence, or illness, or just displaying mortal weakness. I'd recently endured my annual appraisal – my boss made me feel worthless – whereas she is a paragon of perfection, her life all regulated like clockwork. No, nothing so fallible as a wind-up clock. Her life was as controlled as a high integrity computer system: her perfect, business systems analyst – whatever the fuck that is – husband, her perfect kids, Tabitha and Matthew, or whatever they're called, nannies and private education in one of Sheffield's leafy suburbs, walking hand-in-hand in matching hats and neat uniforms. I wouldn't be surprised if there wasn't an actual computer involved, deciding meals on the basis of some carefully devised algorithm for optimal nutrition and linked in to her refrigerator and the Waitrose ordering system, and telling her when was the best time to exercise, and for how long, in order to keep her prominent physical features pert, and to keep her heart in top condition so that the ice didn't melt.

I was brought back to reality by Abdi scraping his chair on the tiled floor and going back to the biscuit tin.

'Don't suppose you've not got any with chocolate on?'

I shook my head, but he rootled round in the tin like he had a vague hope of turning up something more interesting than your standard dunking biscuit.

'You were involved in the Jonathan Yates investigation weren't you?'

'Wasn't that the Brightside Foundries case?'

'Yeah.'

'Nasty accident, that.'

'You think that was an accident?'

'Oh, come on. It's just a turn of phrase – shorthand. Call it what you like: an incident or an industrial crime, I don't give a shit – it makes no difference to how I investigate.'

'I'm just saying there was nothing accidental about molten aluminium showering all over someone. Nothing accidental about the lack of protective clothing or the fact that water got into the feed.'

'I don't need your lecture. But I'll grant you we never did get to the bottom of how water got into the furnace. The police spoke to Mr Yates before he died, in those last few days of his at Pinderfields burns unit, and he said he was directly responsible for checking the feed and drying it out.'

'We spoke to the lads at the foundry who swear that everything was checked over. Jon wasn't daft – he was a clever bloke in fact…'

There was a plop as half a soggy biscuit dropped off into Abdi's mug. 'Pass us the spoon.'

Josh shook his head slowly.

'They say it wouldn't take much water for an explosion like that.'

'No, not much. Imagine what's in this wine glass expanding to fill the space of two wheelie bins in a split second, so, if that tries to escape from the bottom of a furnace full of molten metal, you don't have to wonder at the volcano it produces.'

'So they'd have to have found a way to get a sealed container of water into the furnace?'

'Yes, I suppose. Are you saying Yates was one of yours too?'

'Yes.'

'Shit. This is a bit heavy.'

'Heavy is not the word for it.'

'But the fact that the PPE they were wearing wasn't up to the job – that was not predictable.'

'PPE?'

'Personal protective equipment – flame proof overalls.'

'What? That the one batch supplied to Brightside Foundries wasn't up to spec?'

'We blamed the company for just buying cheaper kit – they had switched suppliers. It had the right labels on but didn't do the job. That's why we prosecuted the supplier too.'

I swirled the wine round the glass, idly watching what the French call the legs – those streaks that form down the sides.

'So, let me get this straight, you reckon David Pitt's death was – and let's just for a minute assume your conspiracy theory is right – that his death was not a one-off? That there is some sort of targeting going on?'

Both Abdi and Josh nodded grim-faced. 'First they tried just blacklisting people, stopping union activists – the ones that were any good – from getting work. Keeping them away from places of work where they could operate effectively. We managed to expose that – shine light on it so that it had to be discussed in Parliament, so that has gone quiet again for now. Do you doubt that they're still at it though? But now they're just looking to exert control in other ways: cutting off funds, or stopping workplace organising. And, if needs be, they'll eliminate them. What were Brightside Foundries and the clothing supplier fined?'

'Twenty grand each.'

'That was paid by a benefactor, did you know that?'

'No, we never get to hear afterwards. It all goes straight to the Treasury.'

'It's the same money just going round in circles, paid out in government loans or interest payments on lucrative Private Finance Initiatives, transferred on in clever financial wheezes or charitable donations, through nod and wink accounting tricks, and ending up being used to pay fines in cases like this. So it all looks like a well functioning system. And if *even you* think we're mad conspiracists, what chance would there be of whistle-blowing to the public and them actually using that information to change the government?'

'But that's exactly what's happening isn't it: with Philpott winning the Labour leadership election – people turning to Labour again – a different sort of Labour – starting to see what the government is up to – seeing through its lies. At last there's someone with an answer not based on nationalism and hatred of others.'

'Very touching. Do you think for one minute the establishment in this country will allow him to get near power? They started off with a well orchestrated campaign to discredit him personally – the way he dressed, the fact he didn't roar out God Save the Queen like an Old Etonian, that he doesn't wear the right kind of tie to the wrong kind of event, that he burps and farts and is caught off camera yawning or picking his nose or eating a burger in the wrong kind of way. When that didn't work because most people just thought it made him look normal – and God forbid we elect someone normal – they start to bombard us with scares over the economy and security, defence – they call up all their mates at The Daily Shyster and keep repeating it until it becomes a truth in itself – because it is said so often it must be true. Even then, if despite all that, this feeble thing that some call democracy lets him in – they will bankrupt the country through the money markets rather than allow him to implement any policies. They'd rather see the country brought to its knees than allow a possibility of a more egalitarian society succeeding. These people have a stake in something higher than single nations – their individual wealth is greater than that of many countries; they don't really have sentimental allegiances to territories, despite their banging on about sovereignty.'

'So who are these shady forces you're up against?' I offered the bottle of wine to them, but both shook their heads so I tipped the rest into my glass.

'That's enough for tonight, eh, Abdi?'

'Yeah.'

'Abdi will call round tomorrow night for that flue pipe, yeah?'

I nodded. They let themselves out, leaving me to knock back the rest of the wine before crashing into bed. I got straight off only to wake an hour or so later with thoughts of plots and conspiracies going round my head, trying to bat them away until I fell asleep again part way through the night.

FOUR

I was chosen because I have all the right attributes. It is the natural order of things – evolutionary biology and all that, you know. We can trace our family tree back through centuries, minor royalty included, back to Roger de Beaubourg who came over with the Conqueror to tame the ghastly Celts, and bring some refinement to the country.

I am Kate Fitzwilliam-Bryce, top of that evolutionary tree – generations of thoroughbred stock, good food, regular exercise through riding and access to deer parks, and avoidance of filthy cramped conditions in cities and mills. Cheltenham College, Oxford PPE, and a rowing blue. Blonde hair, blue eyes and fabulous tits according to the fifth in line to the throne: but then, his bod's none too shabby either.

After Oxford I couldn't bear the thought of idling around the estate – even riding can get tiresome if you do it every day. I was offered a job at Westminster as a researcher to some junior minister or other, but I was far too young to settle down to something so serious, so I thought I'd try my hand at acting – it's all the thing these days: lots of fit young Etonians were at RADA at the same time as me. It was such a hoot – learning all sorts of tricks for getting on in life – such as how to speak like an oik. Oh the irony! I started out perfecting Cockney, the voice coaches we got access to at RADA were fabulous. You see, these actors like Eddie, Owain, or Tom: you wouldn't know just how posh they really are – a few glasses of Pol Roger and the right kind of company and they sound more like Noel Coward than Loki! But, God forbid that a *real* common person ever actually got to act the part of a common person on screen. The thought is just vile. You don't want your on-screen criminals to actually look like real ones: with bad complexions or remnants of Greggs' pasty adhered to their stubbly fizzogs or bacon gristle stuck in their tombstone teeth. Eeugh!

Now, given a bit of practice, I can do Glaswegian, Irish – even vile accents like Black Country, Scouse or Yorkshire. The trick is not to overdo it – it goes without saying that I'd never actually pass for a working class girl – just not ugly or fat enough, obviously, and my skin isn't grey or textured; but even places like Liverpool have areas that are middle class, so that's where I pitch myself – posh-for-Liverpool, posh-for-Brum.

They are so naïve, people from those places – thinking that "posh Scouse" is at the top of the social scale when in reality it is not even halfway up. The Government has done such a great job in hiding those upper echelons, taking us out of the equation altogether. They're happier squabbling amongst themselves for crumbs. To your ordinary scumbag voter we don't exist – we certainly don't for tax purposes – and of course "we're all in it together," "there is no such thing as society," "we're all middle classes these days." Let them have their little vote every five years – let them think their views are important – that we actually give a shit, then we just get on with running things again.

In 1997, when life for me was all Polly Pockets and plaiting my Shetland's mane, apparently it was quite funny seeing them get all excited, thinking that somehow they were in charge. But they were all too scared to actually do anything and we let them have their little gains. The only time we really cocked it up was over the hunting issue – that was Blair's nasty little, stubborn, moralistic streak for you – and his need to throw some scraps to the dogs after his trouble over the Middle East. It was only a temporary hiatus though: we're back hunting with dogs just the same. Of course not actually chasing foxes; oh no, just following a drag. But every now and then the hounds accidentally come across a little ginger fellow – how can we possibly stop them? And who in the police will take it on when every chief constable in the country rubs shoulders with us one way or another? What else are Masonic lodges, country clubs or member-only golf clubs for? – other than to maintain standards.

I digress. I was talking about my favourite subject wasn't I? I am now rather good at moving amongst "ordinary" people – I have had a few successes at rich footballers' parties. They're such a hoot footballers – they just haven't a clue about anything – more money than sense: much, much, more money! In many ways they are the perfect man – loaded, happy to splash it about, especially for a flash of perfect teeth, blonde hair and a nice pair of tits, no strings attached, fit in every sense of the word, and so, so stupid. What's not to like? "Of course, Sophia – it's one of the names I use – any way you like. Have you met Kyle/Fabrizio/Mathias? I even honed my skills by visiting bars in certain parts of London where construction workers hang out, and called myself Shaz – can you imagine it? (This isn't an official RADA assignment, in case you were thinking.) I'd keep it up all the way to the nearest hotel – some of these builders, freed from their vile clothing, and after a scrub down in a Novotel, standing proud over you – you wouldn't know them from a thoroughbred from the first fifteen, until they open their mouths. I have all on not to laugh sometimes at squeaky scouse, heebie-jeebies, or yacky-dahs. So you can't accuse me of being blindly prejudiced, I'll sleep with fine specimens from the lower orders where they exist. Hell! I even had a boy from Sunderland when I was in halls. I was a vital part of his Oxford education you could say. It's good to let some of these people in the through "charitable" work and bursaries and the likes – makes the system more robust and less open to challenge: "you can't say we're elitist – look there's a Geordie, or a black man, for Heaven's sake." And sometimes these people end up being our stoutest defenders – *they* dined at the top table – well they might *think* they did – and so it must be all right.

After RADA, I was a snapped up by Central Office. I guess I'd grown up a bit since graduating. I was approached by George Vernon-Harcourt, no less. Daddy put pressure on me too – he and George senior were old chums – and George is rather dashing, and definitely Prime Minister material – not half so vulgar as the one we've got now. Also the acting jobs didn't come flying in from Hollywood, and the thought of "treading the boards" night after night trying to prove a point was rather tiresome.

I did a bit of work for George on regulatory reform and on trade union modernisation – that's the term we use – we like reform and modernisation, we like to make things "fairer," less of a burden on the taxpayer – when really what we're doing is cutting, and taking a flame-thrower to all those concessions that weak governments have made since 1832. That was called a "reform bill" too. So it's a sweet irony that we are also "reforming" – back to the natural order of things. One by one, going through the remaining areas of control that plebs have wrested from natural birth right: the demise of those disgusting industries: steel, textiles and, above all, coal, have been a real boon in crushing trade unions that got above themselves. Much better spending our efforts on moving money and goods around and buying things cheaper from abroad.

The battleground is now the public sector – where dinosaurs still roam, thinking they're "making a difference" – salving their feeble consciences by professional do-gooding. The sooner the do-gooders crawl back under their stones, and leave people to stand or fall on their own feet the better. It's not a task we can complete overnight – rather than take the risk of sledge-hammering the whole edifice and jeopardising the strategy by it being revealed, we have learnt it is far better to chip away – chip-chip-chip – after a while you don't even hear the chipping noise. It reaches a point where everyone is so dissatisfied with the resulting mess that they're happy to say good riddance – they forget what they've lost, lose heart or are too apathetic – *why should I bother? There's a match on Sky/BT.* – isn't there every night? Ha! *Can't get granny into a decent care home? Never mind it's Manchester versus Chelsea tonight.* Or: *it might never happen to me. Hopefully, everything will still be all right if it does. Why spend money on a pension? It's just like insurance – a waste of money – better putting the odd pound on a lottery ticket.* Ha! Another tax on stupidity.

And of course, now we live in a post-truth society, there is no expectation anywhere that the truth will be told to the swinish multitude: facts and the truth go against the current vibe. Just keep drip-feeding your slogans and sound bites: you can always change your mind after the election and blame somebody else. An awful lot can be forgotten by the hogs before another five years is up; it will be a whole new debate.

It was whilst working one evening in George's office in Portcullis House on some Bill or other to stop lazy civil servants from walking off with what we have got the Mail to report as whopping redundancies, that a man entered without knocking and sat down. He said George had given permission to speak to me, that it was of vital national importance, that I'd get paid handsomely, and would have great fun.

We stayed in a nice little pile in Hertfordshire surrounded by trees and more security than Chequers. The training itself was rather exciting – like being on the set of a Bond movie. There were a few of us selected: two dark blues, a light blue, and a rather nice-looking chap who went to the LSE, via Harrow, who was in line for a baronetcy as soon as his old man did the decent thing. He resisted my charms, so he must have been an up-hill gardener, more's the pity.

We had tutorials on trade union and Labour Party organisation, and lectures from operatives who had held posts in the unions for a number of years, or from policemen and policewomen, some in quite senior positions, who explained how the police operated and how we couldn't always trust the police as some of them were do-gooders and many of the rank and file genuinely believed in concepts like "transparency" and "integrity."

We also did fitness training – not that that posed much of a problem for us trainees given our backgrounds. One finds it somewhat easier to have leisure pursuits when work is more a pastime than a necessity, when not familiar with the opiate of the masses that is a Big Mac, and when congenital deformity doesn't run in the family.

None of us were told what our work was to be – that came later.

We were shown case studies of reds with a history of insurrection and violence – who would stop at nothing until they had spread their corrosive doctrine. We were built up as being vital to holding up the values of our country.

One day a prominent Labour MP came to meet us – I couldn't possibly give you his name – but it came as a shock to us, I'll tell you. It's not like he was one of the well-known anti-Philpott dissenters, either. He was apparently one of the Labour Party members we had got into Parliament in the 97 election. He provided valuable insights into just what Philpott could get up to if he was ever allowed anywhere near the reins of power and just what a threat to our national security he was. This was literally a matter of life and death.

My favourite activities whilst sojourning in Hertfordshire were weapons training – learning to handle a rather gorgeous, and absolutely bloody deadly, little pistol that was not detectable by a metal detector – made with the latest polymer and carbon-nanotube technology – a plastic gun of all things? It wasn't to be our weapon of choice, however: far too obvious – more for self-defence. I also loved the surveillance and counter surveillance stuff – tiny cameras with sound-recording built-in, bugs for relaying telephone conversations, and all the computer stuff – though we were only given the rudimentaries on that – those geeks train for years to do what they do.

All this excitement was punctuated by the occasional game of croquet on the sun-dappled lawns, followed by Pimms on the terrace to the accompaniment of a string quartet. English summertime at its best.

When we returned one morning from our room, George Vernon-Harcourt joined us for breakfast, and with him a distinguished-looking, older lady – she was introduced to us as a Lady Belvedere, an eminent historian. She was, we were told, the leading intellectual behind the Perceval Group. This organisation are named after Spencer Perceval, George said. Had he not been killed, then the era's greatest Prime Minister may have changed the course of history and averted the calamity that befell the nation in the following twenty years. This was to be our entertainment for the day: George and the Dragon, someone quipped, when safely out of earshot. George also went by the name of "Top Cat," apparently. We heard others referred to as Benny, Brains, Spook, and Choo-choo; though we were never introduced to them.

The ballroom was where our classroom was: overlooking the Italianate garden beyond, but my eyes scarcely wandered outside that day. Our purpose was starting to become clearer – no that's not right – it was fulsomely clear from the start that we were not some crack group of Rotarians heading out into the constituencies to assist in voter registration or organising telephone canvassing. No, what George and the Dragon did was remove any remaining doubt we might have had about the importance of our work for the future of Great Britain. This was about preventing widespread disorder on the streets, maintaining the rule of law, stopping rioting and looting as was seen in the 1980s or in 2011. That is where Philpott would take us if the poll ratings trends were allowed to continue. It would also finally put an end to that odious Wee Jimmy Cranky look-alike and her heathen attempts to undermine the good work that The Confessor started at Berwick and Dunbar.

They gave us a fundamental belief, a truth that lies behind it – a faith, almost, in the principle of heredity – that this nation has suffered immensely from allowing people, who were too feeble-minded to understand difficult concepts, to have power and influence over decisions. They had an inspiring vision of the country run once again by a monarch and a selected group of people appointed to posts, not on the whim of some shift in popular mood, but on ability and capacity to make firm decisions and stick to them without the short-termism of a five-year political beauty pageant where empty-headed MPs were chosen on their ability to spout blandishments, avoid direct questions, and not look a goon when a rapid-fire camera was used, and who had no skeletons in closets. The fifth in line to the throne was mentioned as being on board with these concepts, and I smiled at my memories of that pool party outside Oxford. It was glossed over how the obstacles of the first and second in line were to be dealt with before such a regency could be established.

After three months of this I was going stir-crazy – the whole of the three months we had been confined to the grounds – never getting closer than the secure zone at the perimeter of the estate. We were well fed and looked after, of course, but it all felt surreal: like we were in this world but not of it. I suppose it is only what they feel on the International Space Station or on an Antarctic base over winter – or is it summer?

But then it got much worse. In the middle of the night I was woken by the light coming on suddenly and several men entering my room. I screamed, but, before I could act, I was pinned down, gagged, had my hands and feet bound, and a sack put over my head.

'Don't fucking struggle, or you'll end up hurt,' one of them said.

I was picked up roughly and carried out of the room. I was put in the back of a van – it must have been – and driven away. I don't think we could have gone very far because about five minutes later we stopped and I heard men get out and open the door – it was one of those sliding doors. It was cold – I was still in my nightwear and it got colder as I was put onto a cold tile floor. The sack was taken off my head and I blinked and look around me as I lay on my side. It was some sort of factory unit – I could see the stainless steel legs of tables or workbenches. I tried to think who could have got access to the house and done this. My bladder ached but I didn't want the added humiliation of wetting myself.

'Ok, get her seated.'

'Right don't struggle or try to escape or I'll have to hurt you,' a man said as he approached.

My gag was removed: 'Who the hell are you,' I said.

'Shut up and do as you're told. We ask the questions,' the first man said. Their accents were neutral – southern, but neutral – like a BBC newsreader, nothing remarkable about them.

I had my legs freed and was pulled upright, then I was made to sit on a plastic chair – one of those awful ones with moulded arms and legs that you see in cheap cafes. My ankles were bound to the chair legs and my wrists rebound to the armrests with silver tape.

The man who had stood back and watched, as I was picked up off the floor, approached me and struck me across the side of my face with the flat of his hand.

'If you are going to kill or rape me, get on with it,' I said.

'Come on, Kate, there's no need for that. That is not what this is about.'

'It's Catherine to you. Or, better still, Miss Fitzwilliam-Bryce. And what is *this* about?'

'We want you to tell us what you know about the Perceval Group, and what your assignment is.'

'I have no idea what you're talking about.'

'Don't be a silly girl, we know why you've been at that house for the last three months.'

'Then you don't need me to tell you, do you? Go to hell!'

'OK, Lance. She'll need the stuff to loosen her tongue.'

The other thug went over to a metal bench to one side of the factory unit. On it was what looked like an instrument case. Not unlike those that some of the surveillance equipment we'd played with had been in. He flipped the catches and took out a small ampoule and a syringe. He filled the syringe, up-ended it, tapped it, and squirted out the air – just like in one of those films – in fact it could have been a film set. I struggled against the bindings on my arms and legs. I hated needles.

'Don't you put that fucking thing near me.'

'Then tell us what you know.'

'Fuck off.'

The thug came over with the syringe. I figured I might as well go out fighting, so managed to overturn the chair. My right leg came free and, despite bare feet, I managed to land him a blow on the leg. But then both men overpowered me and I felt the needle prick my leg.

I waited to start feeling woozy, or for a hit like cocaine or heroine to come over me, but nothing happened.

Then I heard a door open and some footsteps approach me across the tile floor.

'Well done, Kate. That was impressive.' It was George.

'What the fuck? You bastard!'

'Now, now. It was for your own good. You have now experienced worse than you'll ever get, and passed with flying colours. That hypodermic was just saline by the way – nothing to worry about. The boys will drive you back now and let you get back to bed.'

'Why have you singled me out for this treatment?'

'Don't worry. Everyone is given equal treatment round here – they will all be a bit bleary-eyed in the morning. Goodnight, Kate. Sleep tight.'

'You think I'll get back to sleep after that, you bastard?'

'Well, at least rest, then. You learn about your assignment tomorrow.'

FIVE

I t was a bit of a slow start on the morning after Josh and Abdi's uninvited visit – I didn't feel so good after my disturbed night, and I don't suppose a whole bottle of red wine helped. I decided to leave the car at home and get the bus in. My boss had probably been at her desk for at least an hour when I got in – she glanced up over the partition as if to acknowledge my late arrival, without actually acknowledging me. 'And a very good morning to you too, Patricia,' I muttered under my breath.

When I logged onto my computer an appointment flashed up on my calendar. She had booked a KIT meeting with me at ten – a *KIT meeting*, for those who are lucky enough not to know is a "keep in touch" meeting – one of the many such nauseous little pieces of Civil Service jargon – maybe it goes wider than the Civil Service, but modern senior civil servants are particularly in love with these linguistic abominations. "Across the piece" is another favourite – you even get idiots who attempt to use the jargon and come out with "across the piste" – but that bastardisation of a neologism might just appeal to Patricia and her little Chamonix-downhill-darlings. Everything has to be "strategic," every discussion has to include the words "going forward," "granularity" and "impact." I still have no idea what "segmentation" is, despite having ticked it off in a number of games of bullshit bingo that the lower ranks devise to get us through conferences without going insane. Anyhow, why she couldn't just pop over and say "Mitch, can we have a chat to see how things are going?" No, she has to populate my calendar with a half hour slot of her precious time for a "KIT meeting."

There was no point getting into anything so I fetched a mug of tea and got out my old notebooks – I wanted to refresh my memory as to the Brightside Foundry case.

There were records of interviews of all the witnesses: those that had worked alongside Jon Yates. He was the main furnaceman in charge of loading the furnace. These furnaces were rather old, oil-fired furnaces that had a feed opening at about chest height – Jon had never stood a chance really. It was surprising he was even alive when the ambulance took him away. But that's the thing with burns injuries – the removal of your skin often doesn't kill you outright. You die days later from toxic overload in your body as it fails to cope.

My notes said that the scrap aluminium was brought in and sorted, then cut up and held in a warehouse out of the weather. This scrap: old car wheels, window frames, drinks cans, you name it, was mixed with aluminium ingots, according to the grade required – brought in from smelters and stored in another building on pallets. It really was hard to see how water could have entered the furnace. It was assumed that something like a piece of piping had got through – the very fact it had, proved the system was inadequate. The possibility of sabotage had never crossed my mind. Could it really be used as a way to target an individual? If there was anyone so devious they would need to know exactly which material was going to be charged, and when – otherwise all their efforts could go to waste and they'd get the wrong chargeman. They'd need access to the shift rotas and the stock control, then be in a position to access the shop floor to tamper with the feed. You could just throw a sealed tube containing water into the scrap pile but how would you know whether the particular piece of scrap metal would get shovelled up and put in the stillage that was destined for Jon's furnace?

What someone might be able to work out was where the ingots were heading – particularly if you knew that a particular grade was required on a certain day. I checked my notes from the interview with the warehouse manager. There were perhaps up to twenty pallets of ingots at any one time – they came in at one end and were taken away to the furnaces – like in a queue – from the other. That way, any moisture on them from transportation would have dried off before it was their turn for the furnace, and it was easier for forktrucks to offload at the warehouse entrance. You could almost guarantee which pallet of ingots would be used for any particular batch.

At half a minute to ten, I saw my boss move from her desk to the meeting room she had booked. I got my pen and notebook in which to jot down her words of wisdom – I never looked at them again, but it kept her off my back – made it look better for me. She was sat waiting with her notes of our previous meeting in front of her – "What we agreed last time" – though in reality it was just what she had said last time and I had had to just nod. There is little point in adopting a more resistant approach.

She had a print-out of the work I had done so far: how many visits, how much of that time I had cost-recovered or charged back to the companies inspected, how many notices I had served, the status of my investigation work, how much sick leave taken – half a day for a hangover, after my girlfriend walked out on me, and I'd spent the evening in the Woodseats Palace – how many minutes on average I spent in the gent's – that's a joke – I think. Though I bet she resents the fact there's one room in the building where she can't keep tabs on me.

'This is a satisfactory performance. So far.' Note the pause before the "so far." She can never bring herself to describing anything I do as ever being "good" – heaven forbid any stronger adjective. Everything I do could have been done better if she done it herself.

'Thank you.' I made eye contact with her and tried to maintain it, but had to look away, back down at my notebook.

'Keep it up. I think this places you firmly in the centre of the Performance Wave.'

I couldn't be bothered to argue – and trust me you really don't want to delve into trying to understand what a "performance wave" is. I'd worked bloody hard so far, and "satisfactory" and "firmly in the centre" was all I got. She only handed out accolades and "exceptional performance" awards to her favourites – which seemed to involve being more "happy clappy" around her, rather than getting on with the job. But it is not just *what* you do, but *how* you do it. Whether you demonstrate "positive behaviours." Like something out of an old public school: where you had to thank the schoolmaster for thrashing you.

'What work have you got coming up?'

'I've got those landlords to chase up for their gas safety certificates – they're choosing not to reply to my letters, I think. I'll see if I can get out to track them down and get statements off the tenants if needed. I also need to go back to Brightside Foundry for a post-prosecution review.'

'Has that not been done yet?' – a note of disdain in her voice.

'No, I've had other priorities: that we discussed.' I looked up at her again, and like Reggie Perrin's hippo – it was one of my dad's favourites, that he had on box-set – there flashed in my mind an image of her naked. Don't get me wrong I don't do this with female colleagues – I'm no misogynist. I don't obsess about the female form. It's just my boss. I don't want to. I really don't. It's just there, like a bad daydream – a "daymare?" I can't imagine her as a sexual being at all – it's a perverse trick of my mind. I suppressed a shudder.

'I can ask one of the others to do that visit then, if you're busy. Max is looking for development opportunities – and carrying out a management systems inspection is on his list of competencies…'

'No, I'd rather go myself – it would be more efficient than spending a lot of time briefing Max. I'll get straight onto it.'

'Very well. So we can agree that you'll keep making progress with your targets and will close-out those gas cases and "open" investigations. I don't need to e-mail you?'

'No. I have made a note of it, thanks.'

I got up to go, not wanting to spend any longer in her presence than I had to.

'Crack on,' I said, as if to sound enthusiastic and excuse myself.

People start to drift away from the office at about four thirty, the main exodus at five. I carried on entering data on the computer to feed the insatiable machine. Still my boss sat there. I went downstairs to see if there was anyone on the floor were the evidence room was located. I checked the clock on the wall – five thirty. The last person was logging off and putting things away. I went back up. My boss was still sat typing away. I couldn't risk being caught with the flue pipe.

I was no longer doing anything useful, I shuffled papers about and put things away, went to wash my mug and sat back down. She appeared to be getting ready to go. I logged off and sat staring at a file. I heard the little jingle from her computer shutting down. She put on her pashmina scarf, got up and left without saying good evening. As I headed downstairs the cleaner was making her way up to the next floor.

'Good night,' I said, and got a smile back.

'Yes, to you too, love. You got anything planned for the evening?'

'No. Quiet night in again I should imagine.'

I saw, through the window, my boss lifting the boot of her car in the car park. It was then I realised I'd come in on the bus – how stupid when I was on a mission to steal. I couldn't be seen with evidence bags. I went to the kitchen and found a roll of black bin bags under the sink and pulled two off. The key cabinet was locked, but I had the code written in my diary as part of the emergency plan: if we were called out to an incident out of hours, we might need access. I got the evidence room key and went in, shutting the door behind me. The flue pipe was still where I'd last seen it so I shoved it in a bin bag and put another over the top, quickly left the room and put the key back in the cabinet. As I entered the foyer of the building to head out of the front entrance, the door to the car park opened. My boss came through in a rush. I quickly moved the large object wrapped in black bags behind my back.

'Forgotten my laptop charger, and there's an open evening at the High School tonight.'

I shuffled towards the entrance door trying my best to look nonchalant with four feet of flue pipe in bin bags behind my back. She looked at me from the staircase and hurried on. I pressed the door release and once out ran to the bus stop on adrenaline.

At about eight that evening, there was a knock at the door and the grinning face of Abdi appeared when I opened it.

'You got it?'

'Yes, but it wasn't easy. I nearly got caught off my boss.'

'Did he see anything?'

'*She.* No, and if she did, all she saw was me with something wrapped in bin bags.'

'Will they notice it missing?'

'I doubt it. Not for a while. I want to get it back as soon as I can now, though.'

'Okay, I'll see if I can return it tomorrow night.'

'I was just putting the kettle on. Do you want one?'

'Yeah, okay. Ta.'

'Take a seat.'

He didn't. I got the decent Pollards' coffee out of the freezer – one of my few luxuries – and got out the cafetière.

'I've been thinking about the Jon Yates case. It's hard to see how it could have been done.'

'How's that?'

'Well the obvious place to try to hide a container of water would be in the scrap feedstock – but you never know when or if it would get charged into the furnace and it might not get the right person. The only thing you can pretty much guarantee going into a known batch is a solid ingot.' I got the biscuit tin and the sugar cubes and we sat down.

'Could it be that? An ingot?'

'No because they're solid.'

'What if they weren't?'

'They are. Unless you put in a fake one?'

'That could be it then?'

'It would be tricky to see how that was done unless you'd got all the right equipment.' I dunked a ginger-nut. 'I suppose, perhaps, you could hollow one out? It would also need someone with access to the daily work orders.'

'Can you find out anything, do you think? I can't see them leaving an operative in place for long after a successful hit – so it would likely be someone who left soon after, if it was an inside job that is.'

'It's got to be an inside job, surely? It would be hard, otherwise – getting access to the computer system.'

'That's the easy bit. The hardest thing would be knowing who was on shift, unless that was computerised, and getting the dodgy ingot in place. Most likely a placed operative. Too much scope for error otherwise. So, do you reckon you can you find out any more?'

'I was already wondering that.'

'Nice one.'

I watched him dunk a sugar cube in the black coffee; the brown liquid seeping upwards. He then crunched on it before getting another one. This time he held it until it dissolved. The backs of his hands were hairy – and his fingers below the knuckles. I imagined he was pretty hairy individual all round – unless he followed the fashion for waxing. Didn't look like it from the hairs sticking over the top of his t-shirt and up his forearms.

'Do you live local?' I asked.

'Yes, in Sheffield.'

'I meant round here? Come on you've got the pipe, you can trust me.'

'Over at Shiregreen.'

'Married?'

'No. I share a flat with a cousin. It's not as nice as this,' he said, gesturing around him.

'Yeah, it's all right. Bit expensive, now I'm paying off the mortgage on my own. It don't leave me much beer and skittles money after I've paid my bills.'

'So, what happened? You said *now* you're paying on your own.'

'The usual. She walked out on me. Said I took her for granted. Didn't pay enough attention to her. Didn't take her out clubbing, wouldn't go with her to Meadowhall every Saturday afternoon. I ask you, Saturday afternoons at Meadow-hell, instead of being at the football. It takes a special kind of bloke to want to spend time watching someone try on shoes rather than watch footy.'

'Sounds like you're better off out of it, mate.'

'I dunno, maybe. There can be advantages, but y' know…'

'Yeah, I suppose… Good coffee this – be better with milk.'

'I was weaned when I was ten months old, ta.'

'Not even chanar dalna curry?'

'Some things aren't worth it when you know what goes into them.'

'Boring though.'

'Not really. Thought it was you that was the man of principle… Look, are you going to tell me more about who these shady people are you're up against?'

'Sometime maybe. I'll see what Josh says.'

'Is he your boss or something?'

'No, we're just comrades – some things need a democratic approval, let's say. Thanks for the coffee and for the present.' He picked up the bin-bagged parcel.

'Oh, try and open the evidence bag without destroying it too much. I don't suppose anyone will look too closely at the seal, but just in case.'

'Don't worry, see you.'

'Yeah. See ya.' I picked up my jacket and headed straight out after him to the Palace to see if there was anyone there for a game of pool and a jar or two.

*

The following evening I got back from work and set to on a chickpea salad for tea whilst listening to the six o'clock news on the kitchen radio. A scandal had been uncovered involving two Tory ministers having bypassed NHS waiting lists for their families. This had ostensibly been done through their private health insurance but a whistleblower at a London hospital had revealed there had been interference with the waiting lists to allow these private operations to be carried out in the NHS hospital, using facilities not available in the private hospital – and at the expense of a more urgent case. One patient had died having had their kidney transplant delayed as a result. The prime minister had suspended the individuals pending an enquiry, but more such abuses were being hinted at: that this wasn't such a one off. It wasn't going to be easily hushed up. Attempts had been made to find the whistleblower to interview her, but she had been found dead in her garage – a presumed suicide.

I had just sat down to eat when the door opened and Abdi walked in.

'That's all right, mate. Don't feel you have to knock. Just come in, why don't you.'

'Cheers, mate.'

He nodded to the radio: 'You heard the news?'

'What? Those bastards queue jumping? This government's falling apart, man. I tell ya.'

'No. The whistleblower: a UNISON convenor.'

'Yeah: committed suicide. Terrible. I guess it's hard being a whistleblower. No one likes a snitch. What… ?'

Abdi was looking at me shaking his head. 'I had you down as bright. Two plus two makes what?'

'Oh… not suicide. Shit. Not another?'

'Looks like it – anyhow I can't stop,' he said. 'Got a meeting to go to. Here's the pipe back.'

'And?'

'Nothing on it. Not a single print. It has been wiped clean.'

'Really?'

'Yep. Don't you think that backs up our theory?'

'Well, I suppose it does seem odd. Who wiped it clean? Whoever installed it?'

'Or the police.'

'Why would they do that?'

'If only you knew what they did get up to in the name of upholding Britain's values. Look, if you can find out any more about what happened to Jon, we're cool with that.'

'I'll see.'

'Here, take this.'

He handed over a cheap Nokia phone.

'It's got my number in the "contacts" – under the name Roger – and that's it. If you need to speak to me use this. Don't put the number in your own phone. Don't ever use it to phone anyone else: is that clear? Lives may depend on it. Possibly your own.'

'What?'

'Just me. Okay? This is important.' He put out his hand, and I shook it.

'Wait, but…'

He looked me in the eye and smiled. 'Got to go.'

The following day was Friday. I decided to go to Brightside Foundries to carry out the inspection before my boss got jittery: now it was on her radar it would become a stick to beat me with. Then I'd call in at the office later on to slip the flue pipe back into the store, when, hopefully, everyone would have gone home.

It was one of those typical summer days in South Yorkshire: grey and wet and breezy. As I pulled into the yard I had to dodge potholes full of water, and a wagon that was being un-sheeted ready to tip scrap. I pulled over by the office block – an old NCB-style, single storey, brick building tacked on to the warehouse. I went into the small entrance area and picked up the filthy-looking phone and pressed 3 for reception as the sheet of paper sellotaped to the wall instructed.

'Can I help you?' A female voice answered.

'I'd like to see the manager. Is it still Mr Edwards?'

'Have you got an appointment?'

'No, it's Mr Miller, from the Health and Safety Executive.'

'He doesn't see people without an appointment. Please e-mail to arrange an appointment if you wish to see Mr Edwards.'

The phone went dead. This was tiresome. I replaced the handset, picked it up again and pressed 3.

'Yes?'

'It's Mr Miller. Just tell him. I don't need to make an appointment. And you should know it is an offence to obstruct a health and safety inspector.'

'I have been told not to let anyone in without an appointment.'

'I've just made one. Now, you had better let him know if you want to avoid getting into trouble.'

'Wait there, I'll tell him.'

I put the phone down this time. At what point in recent years did we go from being a polite society that respected authority to one that treated all public servants and experts with the same level of contempt reserved for traffic wardens? A cult of ignorance that won a referendum and led to a dick-head being elected as leader of the "free world." Post-truth – FFS. Successive governments had been guilty of pedalling the line that entrepreneurs were the most valued members of society and regulators were just parasites or burdens on business. Ministers ridiculed health and safety in public – how can stopping people getting maimed at work ever be a thing to be derided? They softened people up for their bonfires of quangos and cutting of red tape, both of which they – parliament – had created in the first place. The poor entrepreneurs – superheroes of capitalism – slowed by the kryptonite of the civil service pen-pushers with their archaic beliefs in stopping people getting injured at work. Ministers playing to the gallery of Jeremy Clarkson's or Simon Jenkins' rabid rantings about health and safety. Every one of those bastards should be made to come and work for a day in places like Brightside Foundries.

A solemn-looking woman, thirty-going-on-fifty, with hair scraped back so tight in a ponytail that it lifts the wrinkles – a "Barnsley facelift" – unlocked the glass, sliding hatch which opened into the reception area.

'He says to come through.'

I smiled sweetly at her and said: 'Thank you very much, I'm obliged,' in a cheery voice to wind her up.

The hatch shut abruptly, and the door buzzed – I pushed it open. One-nil.

Edwards, the MD, came along the corridor to meet me. Since I last met him on the steps of the Magistrates, he'd grown a beard and greased back his hair, which was longer on top than at the sides. It was a hopelessly failed attempt to look trendy – what is it they call them in the London media? Hipsters? Except Edwards just looked a scruffy sod. Not something you should try when you turn forty – like dancing, or legal highs, or shopping in The Forum. He was the third generation, or something, of his family running the foundry – the business dating back to before the War. His father, I imagined, was an old school businessman: Chamber of Commerce, boring, risk averse, penny-pinching, never investing, squeezing assets and sweating labour, parking his Jaguar outside every day. As a result it was the uncompetitive shambles of a business it is today: still running the same machinery they had in the 60's. His son Jake, probably grew up with pictures of Thatcher or Edwina Currie on his wall, which he got off on, instead of Natalie Imbruglia, All Saints or whatever a normal teenager would have back then.

'Mr Miller. To what do we owe the pleasure?' I shook his outstretched hand. One of those who pumps up and down vigorously when he shakes hands – at least he didn't go for a fist bump.

'It's a routine visit to see how you're getting on. It's something we do after every prosecution. To make sure all the angles have been covered.'

'Shall we go into the factory?'

'In a bit perhaps. Can we sit down first?'

He led me through to his office with its pictures of him and his father, taken at Wednesday matches. Revolting blue and white images, with them as match ball sponsors or whatever. I try hard not to let these sorts of things prejudice me, but these primeval instincts of revulsion are hard to overcome. The man had even got blue, thick-framed specs on. I explained that I wanted to review their management systems – for managing safety standards generally, as well as their scrap handling procedures.

'Of course we don't accept we did anything wrong.'

'That's not what the court found.'

'But there was nothing to say that the water getting in was our fault.'

'Look, I'm more interested in what you've done since to improve things, rather than going over old ground.'

'Well, we got rid of the foreman.'

'Why was that?'

'He was in charge of the operation.'

He tried blaming anyone but himself. Typical of a bully like Edwards to try to rule by fear. To blame the person lowest down – not to accept it was anything the management failed to do. He'd have sacked the poor victim too, no doubt, if a higher authority hadn't intervened. Dig him up so you can sack him, Mr Edwards, why not?

'So you accept there were management failings.'

'I accept that there was a cock-up. Unless it was Jonathan Yates trying to sabotage the plant, or engineer a compensation claim, and it just went wrong.'

'You can't seriously be suggesting that Mr Yates would have done it himself.'

'I'm just saying it's not something I could have done much about. I pay good wages and expect them to do their jobs properly. Either it was deliberate, or the foreman should have kept a better grip on scrap storage and checking procedures. We kept his job open until the court case, to see what was said.'

Good wages! I'd be surprised if any of them were on less than he could get away with. Probably minimum wage. It was not the sort of place you could imagine anyone choosing to work in. And sacking the foreman was clearly a sop to the shareholders – to create the illusion that action had been taken after the event.

I scribbled a few notes. I had to work harder to get him on side with my main objective. Bite the bullet. Deal with the devil.

'Sounds like they were unlucky on Tuesday night,' I said nodding at the blue and white on the wall. 'That new manager, knows his stuff though, eh? Breath of fresh air. They'll be back where they belong soon.'

That hurt. But it worked, and with a few nods as he went on about what a massive club they were, De Canio, Carbone, Waddle, blah blah, it was like we were old pals. Dick-head!

I got him round to discussing what other staff changes there had been.

'Only the foreman. Oh, and we had to replace Jon Yates, of course.'

A disposable asset.

'What about in management? Or the office? Those ordering and dealing with stock control?'

'There was that temp, we had in. Shame she left, if you know what I mean?'

I smiled at him. 'No, how's that?'

'She was not only a looker, but had brains too. I fancied my chances at one point, but…'

'What, not out of your league, surely?'

He laughed along. 'No, we just couldn't give her the responsibility she wanted, short of her becoming a manager. And that is a family preserve. If only…'

'It was her reorganised our raw materials ordering systems and stock control – got it all running through the computer rather than the old filing system my father set up.'

'I don't remember her.'

'I don't know if you met her, you wouldn't have forgotten her if you had.' He made a tit groping gesture with both hands. 'Sharon Walker? Rotherham lass. But can't hold that against her.'

'Sounds like it was a shame she left. Just a temp though?'

'Yeah, from the agency.'

'Which one do you use?'

'Vector Executive Recruitment.'

'So, she left for a better job?'

'I presume so. No idea where she went after.'

'I'd be interested in seeing this computer system – has it reduced the risks of contaminated feed?'

'Well, we only had it up and running since the accident, but it allows full traceability of each consignment of scrap, so we can work with our suppliers if there are any issues. That keeps them on their toes too.'

Despite all the initial bluster, I found they had actually done quite a lot to improve. Scrap was now sorted in batches and each consignment checked, cut up more thoroughly and segregated. It was still just as shitty a job as before for the lads in the foundry: hot, filthy and fumy. I pushed further on extraction systems and on improving the welfare facilities and said I'd write.

I shook Edwards hand again as I left. My new bezzie mate.

'Can I offer you a coffee before you go?'

'No. Thanks. I've got other places to visit.'

Drinking shit coffee out of a Wednesday mug would be the final emetic straw that made this camel vomit.

'Remind me: the name of that foreman, you sacked?'

'Woolard.'

'That's it. I remember. I'll be in touch.'

Woolard. When back in the car I looked through my old notebook from the investigation – Mick Woolard. He had described how the scrap was handled. He couldn't believe how anything could have crept through, that Jon would have missed anything. He was "pernicky" he had said – always use the witnesses own words they taught us. But it was all fairly shambolic in reality – based on custom and practice, luck and judgement, and no forethought. "We'd never had an accident before." Well, alas, gambling on low probabilities finally caught up with you.

The address he'd given me at the time wasn't far away – up at Wincobank; so I drove round. The door was answered by a woman holding a baby on her hip – cigarette in her free hand.

'Is Mr Woolard in?'

'Who wants him?'

'I'm Miller, a factory inspector. I met him when he was at Brightside Foundry – it's not on: what happened to him there.'

'He's at work, love. Shall I tell him you called?'

'No, it's all right. Where is it he works now?'

She gave me the address of a garage not far from Rotherham's old ground.

I approached its floodlight towers: still standing – a forlorn reminder of football's lost soul. A place where the cries of pain and shouts of triumph still echo faintly round crumbling stands and decaying ironwork.

Sheriff Motors was the kind of garage that shouldn't exist any more. Not now that cars no longer seemed to require constant replacements of parts after five years, and they no longer turned into crumbling piles of rust after a few winters of gritted roads: the modern two-pack paints lasting the lifetime of the vehicle. The garage floor was black with oil and muck, and there was an old-fashioned inspection pit.

I'm so used to just walking into places backed up by the warrant in my pocket, that I forget sometimes that normal people look for a visitor entrance, rather than strolling straight into the workshop. I do this even when going to Kwik-Fit for a tyre for my own car. It unnerves people. There was a man working on a vehicle with the wheel off.

'Is Mr Woolard in? Mick?'

'Ah. Yes. Mick. He through the back,' he said in a thick Eastern European accent.

There was a door through to a junk yard at the back. I thought I recognised Woolard sat on an oil drum smoking.

'Mr Woolard. I'm Mitch Miller. I met you following Jon Yates' accident.'

'Oh aye, I remember. How d'y…?'

'Your wife said you work here. Can I say I don't think it's right how they treated you – there was never any blame attached to you – it was the company that failed in its duties. That was made clear at the inquest and in court.'

'Ay, lad. But what's done is done. Best off out on it, I reckon. What can I do yer for?'

'It's just a couple of loose threads following the prosecution that's all. I thought you might be able to help. Do you remember the temp that worked there? Sharon was it?'

'Oh, aye. I remember her. Rose amongst bloody thorns she were. Classier than your average Rotherham lass. You should see 'em round 'ere.' He puffed out his cheeks and blew.

'Can you describe her, this Sharon?'

'I can do better than that, lad. Here…' He took out his phone from his pocket and started flicking at the screen. It's in here somewhere.'

I waited, letting him get on with it.

'There you are. That's 'er.'

He showed me a picture of a blonde-haired woman in her late twenties: fake tan, loads of make-up, pink vest top with a white skirt and white boots. She was getting out of a pale blue Nissan Micra.

'We'd been trying to get her to pose for a selfie with us, me and the lads, so we could wind each other up about who'd got her to be their girlfriend first. But she were having none of it. She turned out to be a bit of a snooty cow. We were only having a laugh. This sneaky one were the best I could do. I were going to get a mate to Photoshop it and have her getting out of my car, or out of my bed with me lying in it or summat. But then she left and I couldn't be bothered. Don't know why I kept the picture, to be honest.'

'Can I see?' I zoomed in on her face. I got my own phone out. 'Do you mind if I…?' I set my phone up to take a photo of the screen.

'I'll send it to you if you want. What's your number'

I gave it him.

'Can I ask what it's about? Is she in bother?'

'No, nothing like that. It's nothing really, like I said, just a loose end my boss wanted tying off – a bit fussy my boss.' He threw back his head a little – like that was enough of an explanation.

SEVEN

I spent the rest of the afternoon on more routine work – following up a complaint at a waste recyclers, and chasing the whereabouts of a landlord who variously went under the name of Mohammed, Ahmed or "Faz." It was nearly six o'clock when I pulled into the office car park. I went in to check the route to the evidence room was clear before putting the flue pipe back where I found it.

I sent Abdi a text using the phone he'd given me. "Something turned up. Fancy a pint?"

No sooner had I put it back in my pocket than it beeped. "Yours for 8."

I stopped off at the Co-op at the garage for stuff for tea and watched the end of the local news and *The One Show* while I did mushroom risotto and some fruit salad. It was just gone eight o'clock when he showed up, in baggy grey jogging pants and matching hoodie, ridiculously big trainers and a baseball hat.

'I was just going to the pub. You coming?' I said.

'What you got for me? Can't we just stay here?'

'I'll only talk to you over a pint.' I smiled at him. I wanted to feel in control – see what he was really like.

I asked him what he'd been up to as we walked down the street on to Chezzy Road.

'Working since early.'

'What is it you do?'

'Taxi-ing.'

'Does that pay well?'

'Not really, it seems to get harder to make a living out of it without working all hours. But there's just me to keep.'

'No family?'

'My mother lives in Nottingham with my sister and her husband.'

'I wish mine lived with my sister. As it is, all the guilt falls to me.

'What are you having?' I said when we got to the bar.

'Just a Diet Coke.'

'Is that it?'

'I'm not supposed to drink alcohol?'

'What for religious reasons?'

'Yeah, but it's more that I don't want to be seen to be drinking. It could draw attention. I wouldn't normally even come in a pub.'

We sat down in a quiet corner and I told him about the woman Sharon at the foundry. I saved the photo for my punch-line.

'You've done well. Very well. I'll need a copy of that picture.'

'I'll send it to you.'

'No, best not. Can I take it?'

'No, it's my phone.'

'I'll bring it back first thing in the morning.'

'Not first thing – it's Saturday. I have no intention of getting up before nine.'

'OK. Nine then.'

I shook my head and sighed, then handed it over.

He flashed me a smile. 'Cheers. You coming?'

'Nah. I'll stop for the second half,' nodding at the screens in the bar showing the Sunderland – Liverpool game: an end of season survival battle for the Black Cats.

I shook his hand and patted him on the shoulder in a sort of "man-hug."

I took the remains of my pint through and looked for a seat. It was full in the bar, but for a stool at a table where a girl sat on her own. Dark haired, very attractive – a class above the usual kind of girl who came in here: sophisticated-looking – like she had been teleported into The Big Tree from some wine bar on Eccie Road. She had one of those familiar faces – perhaps she worked in one of the shops or somewhere.

'Is anyone sat here?'

'Not any more, pet. The bastard's fucked off and left me, so you are welcome to it.' The voice that came from her mouth wasn't quite what I expected. 'Has *your* boyfriend left you an' all pet?' She nodded to where I had been sat with Abdi.

'Boyfriend?' I could feel my cheeks redden. 'Abdi? – he's just a mate. Not that I'm…'

'No, sorry. I thought… No offence.'

'Look, I'll sit somewhere else.'

'Don't be daft. There is nowhere else. I'm sorry I'm just a bit blunt sometimes. That's why I'm sat here on my own, I guess. I told him what I thought of his mother.' She threw her head back as she laughed and I could see all her top teeth and the back of her throat. 'Look I'll get you another pint to apologise. What you having?'

Her laugh was infectious – I was disarmed.

'Go on then: Speckled Hen.'

I watched her at the bar, flirting with the lad who was serving. She returned with two pints and smoothed down her tight little black skirt as she sat. She was very shapely.

'Here you go, pet. I'm Jade, by the way.' She pronounced it "Jay-ud."

'Mitch.'

'Pleased to meet you, Mitch.' She offered her rather nicely manicured hand.

'They your team then? Sunderland?' I nodded towards the screen, as the teams took to the pitch.

'Aye. Right little Sherlock. Haway, let's get one back, eh lads?'

Sunderland did pull one back about ten minutes in – a somewhat jammy deflection that wrong-footed the keeper. It was always quite easy to support the team in red and white. I fetched us another pint. She sat closer to me now, our knees occasionally making contact. We didn't say much – she wasn't one of those girls who just pretend to like football as part of her ladette image and constantly spouts inane crap throughout the game and stops you concentrating. Her only comments were pertinent to the game: about movement off the ball and creating space. As she leaned in to say something I got a whiff of citrus or bergamot from her hair, mixed with the hoppy smell of her breath.

There were chances both ends, neither team fully asserting themselves. Then, when the Columbian Sunderland striker banged a goal in from outside the box, she gave me a peck on the cheek in celebration. I'd not been expecting that: that Columbian would have got a kiss from me for the result his goal produced. I don't tend to hit it off with girls straight away. I'm more of a coarse fisherman than a hook-a-duck kind of bloke. Sitting for bloody hours in the cold, wondering, getting little nibbles, then the long slow process of reeling them in gently in the hope they won't jump off the hook, which they usually do.

She turned her interest to me after the final whistle, only occasionally looking back at the screen when replays of yellow card incidents or penalty shouts were shown, but ignoring the *Sky* pundits blather. She worked as a social media analyst, or something, a job which seemed to involve playing on Facebook or Instagram all day for the clients in her "portfolio."

'Bloody hell – what happened to proper jobs: where you have to graft all day for a living?'

'Ah, but to do it right takes brains and skill – it's where the money is now: online. Have the wrong profile and you'll end up like British Home Stores. Young people have no brand loyalty – they go where it's cool right now – not where it was cool yesterday.'

'No money to be made in comfy pants.'

'Exactly. You wouldn't see me in comfy pants.'

'Oh yeah?'

'Well if you play your cards right… And let me guess you're a boxer-short kind of feller.'

I smiled. 'Not saying.'

'Is that a challenge?' I smiled again. She bit her bottom lip.

'Go on then, get your coat.'

I stood up. 'It's not cold. I didn't bring one.'

She playfully took hold of my arm as she got to her feet. I couldn't believe my luck. She nestled in to me as we headed up to mine.

I wished I tidied up a bit before coming out – I'd left everything out on the side from cooking my tea, bits of newspaper lying around. And, I hated to think what state I'd left the bedroom in – if I got that lucky.

'Do you fancy a coffee?'

'What you got?'

'I've got instant, or proper stuff. I only keep the instant for plumbers and the like – and my mother when she comes round.'

I made a cafetiere and we sat chatting at the kitchen table. She told me about her parents in South Shields – her dad worked in an engineering firm in the Team Valley and her mother was a teaching assistant. She got into Sheffield Hallam University and had stayed on in the city after graduating, as many students do.

'You know Sheffield has more students that stay behind after their degree than anywhere else?'

'I heard that.'

'It gets under your skin, somehow, this place.'

'I've mates who were in to climbing who wouldn't leave after, just because of that – turned down lucrative jobs in the City for some big lumps of granite.'

'Millstone grit.'

'Yeah, whatever.'

She finished her coffee and lent across to kiss me full on the lips. Her mouth was warm and tasted of coffee with a hint of berries from her lip-gloss. I was lost. Nothing else mattered, or ever had.

'Come on then boxer-shorts-boy – you going to show off your paisley-print, or is it tartan?'

She was unbelievable. Not the sort of girl to be demure or passive. She was fully in control – in control of what happened and what did not, and it was like I'd handed over the keys and the passcode to my own body. It was me who had to lie back and think of England: I had to concentrate bloody hard so as not to get too carried away – starting with goalkeepers from Fraser Forster and Joe Hart, going all the way back through Robinson, James, to Shilton, Clemence and Banks. I was so turned on I was able to go again not long after. I couldn't remember the last time that that had happened – certainly never while I was sharing a house and a bed full time.

EIGHT

I was woken when the sun shining on the curtains finally penetrated my consciousness. I instantly remembered the night before and reached over to the other side of the bed. It was empty. Sitting up made my head pulse – one too many beers. I pulled on some jeans and went out onto the landing. There was no sound. I went downstairs – that was empty too. The kettle was not even warm. There was a jiffy packet on the mat by the back door – my phone – posted through by Abdi. That was all. No note, nothing. The only sign she had been was the mug she had washed and placed on the draining rack. At least it was Saturday.

I watched United snatch defeat from the jaws of victory again that afternoon – yet another end-of-season teaser where minor hopes are rekindled then snuffed out – some sort of crap, dance of the seven veils, where right at the end you realise the dancer had a boiler suit on all along.

I spent the rest of the evening with cousin Pete and a few of the lads we've hung about with since school. A mostly liquid tea to supplement the half-time packet of crisps – funnily enough none of the pies at Bramall Lane are vegan – that and a falafel wrap from the takeaway on London Road when we left the Cremorne to get the bus back up the hill.

On the bank holiday Monday I had arranged to pick up my mother from the sheltered housing and take her out. She was waiting with her coat on when I arrived. I was only a few minutes late. I had on shorts and a T-shirt.

'Won't you be too hot mother?'

'Oh no. It's not that warm out. Not that I've been out much lately, but you all have such busy lives, I suppose.'

On the way to Hope Valley Garden Centre she told me all about her marvellous daughter and the grandchildren and the new conservatory for their lovely home in Bristol. My sister thinks a weekly phone call and a visit at Christmas equates to everything I have to do on the spot, here in Sheffield. She also sends mother

53

pictures on Facebook. Yes, my mother has a Facebook account –
that I had to set up – and which I have to go round and sort out
when it needs the password entering again, and, for whatever
reason, she can't get straight on it from the iPad I bought her. It's all
she uses it for: to keep a check on the upwards trajectory of my
darling sister, her hot-housed offspring, and her *anker of a
husband. That's a "b," by the way, in case you wondered.

We wandered around slowly looking at the alpines, mother
holding onto my arm, her stick supporting her on the other side.
Then we went to the cafe for tea and cake. As we sat down my old
Nokia phone buzzed in my shorts pocket. The text read: You free
tonight? I replied with a: Yes, and got back a: Bishops House, 8.00.

Despite living so close to it, I had not visited the house since we
studied the Elizabethans at school, so I had a wander around the
outside. On my second lap I found Josh waiting by the entrance.

'I was expecting Abdi.'

'You'll have to put up with me instead.'

I shook his hand.

'How was the garden centre?'

'How did you know?'

'We can track your signal: just to be on the safe side.'

'Bloody hell – so now I'm being spied on? What's this about?'

'I'll tell you, come on.'

We went to sit on a bench at the top of the park, overlooking the
city as the sun started to go down over the hills to our left. Down
below, the domes of the mosque, the spires of churches, and the
equally hallowed-ground of Bramall Lane. Beautiful it was. If only it
were Jade I was with. Not a squeak from her: I'd not even had
chance to swap numbers with her. Was I just a one-night shag for
her – as therapy for her boyfriend having stormed out on her?
Mitch Miller, therapist to the sad and washed up. That's me.

'So what is it you want?' I asked.

'Did you hear about that journalist who has gone missing?'

'You mean the Newsnight one?'

'Well, he's freelance, but he has been on Newsnight. There are
still some editors with integrity.'

'Wasn't he into the blacklisting thing?'

'Yes, he's been doing a lot of digging and getting very close.'

'To what?'

Josh paused and looked out over the city as some pigeons reeled in a flock over the roofs.

'Look,' I said, 'if you want my help, or something, you've got to let me know what's going on, otherwise it's over. You know you can trust me – I put my job on the line to help you – you've had the flue pipe and a photo of that blonde lass. Just who are you, and who is it you are up against?'

'Okay, but this is serious – mention it to anyone and I'll have to kill you.'

I laughed; then seeing his dead-pan face, realised that wasn't the usual clichéd joke. 'Shit, you mean that.' He nodded. 'Okay, shoot.'

'Well you sort of know who we are – a group of right-minded trade unionists and assorted lefties. None of us are particularly hard line. We support the Labour Party under Philpott – we're democrats who believe in telling the truth to the electorate and trusting their judgment. The trouble is they're not told the truth and are manipulated. Like during the referendum.'

'Yeah, I understand all that. I don't want a lecture on Marxism.'

'We are not really an official organisation. Not that we could be, you understand, but we do have an executive committee.'

'And how is it funded?'

'Surprisingly, not all rich people are fascists. We have one or two individuals who have come by money and want to put it to the cause of true democracy.'

'So what is it called, this organisation thing?'

'It doesn't really have a name, officially, but the shorthand we use is "The Fourth Way." '

'You mean like *the third way*?'

He hissed like I'd mentioned the horned man in the smoky house. 'Yeah, it was a joke name to start with, ironic – given what the party stood for back then and how it was really under the control of the establishment. Some refer to it as "the Project" or "Plan D." '

'And who are these people you're up against?'

'It's an old boys' network and goes by the name of the Perceval Group – named after Spencer Perceval.'

I nodded, vaguely remembering stuff about Perceval from something I'd read or seen on a documentary.

'Was he the one that got shot?'

'That's him.'

'So this group…'

'They work slightly outside of the main establishment but maintain a toe in the Tory Party – quite how far in their poisonous tendrils reach is not clear. They are well organised and believe above all in heredity. They are basically monarchist fascists who dream of glory days that never existed – rule by kings and barons. They are deeply nationalistic, but also have links with neo-nazi groups all over Europe and America.'

'So you think it's them that killed Dave Pitts and Jon Yates?'

'We know it. That woman you identified for us – we know she has some links. We have a mole within the Perceval Group, an Old Etonian who has seen the light – a rare breed – someone whose brain actually functioned, who escaped in-breeding and put his education to good use by actually thinking. He recognised her as someone he met in the Oxford University Young Conservatives – not "Sharon from Rotherham." '

'Shit! So it was murder?'

'Yes, this confirms what was just a theory. So your work has been invaluable.'

'And what happens next? Can you take it to the police?'

'The police! You're kidding? Fuck's sake, Mitch, you've still a lot to learn. They would laugh at us, and send some thugs round to shut us up. No, we've got to be smarter than that.'

'How do you mean?'

'This is a fight to the death. They are systemically cutting off the root to kill the organism. Working away, undermining Philpott's credibility and hunting out scandal whether it's real or not – discrediting his supporters if there is the slightest whiff of anti-semitism or impropriety. And because the left is generally scandal free – made up of decent honest people – there isn't much to go on, so they look to eliminate certain key people who form a crucial hub of support. By taking out one effective, irreplaceable campaigner you can neuter dozens more who relied on that one individual: like Dave, or Jon, or Mark Tyler, the journalist.'

'That Yorkshire MP?'

'Probably not linked. But they all swim in the same swamp.'

'So, where does that leave you, the Fourth Way or whatever?'

'We have to respond. Get them to back off – mutually assured destruction.'

'What?'

He stopped speaking as a man walked past with a greyhound on a lead.

He resumed. 'For every one of ours, we take one of theirs.'

'Bloody hell.'

'Can you think of a better way?'

'That's being as bad as them.'

'Yes, but we have no other way of stopping them. They don't care how many they kill through direct actions or indirectly through their policies, but as soon as they see their ranks fall they sit up. It is happening already.'

'Sharon from Rotherham, or whoever she is?'

'Target number two.'

'Not one?'

'No. That place is reserved for someone special. Something I can't discuss.'

I gazed out over the town as the sky faded and lights started turning on over the city. 'Bloody hell, what a mess this country's in.'

'Always has been, mate. Always has been.'

'And this journalist fella, Tyler?'

'He's not just been looking at the blacklisting issue for Newsnight. He's been looking to expose the Percevals and had some information from an undercover job, we believe. He told his colleague he was off to a MacFarlane construction site in Southwark to meet a contact, but he never returned. There's a pattern emerging here, don't you think? Deaths occurring in workplaces or covered by the Health and Safety at Work Act?'

'I suppose. People have long said that if you want to commit the perfect murder the best way is to employ them. There is no public outcry when people get killed at work – the public accept it – they tolerate a few hundred deaths a year to keep the wheels of capitalism turning – just fuel for the machine. Look at what happened when those lads got buried under the power station, those Gambians in Birmingham, or worse still that building that collapsed in Glasgow – the media hardly bats an eyelid. And if you add to that how successive governments have screwed the Inspectorate: we're lucky to have the resources for more than a cursory investigation of a death. The police will throw teams of officers onto a murder, with forensics and helicopters, the lot. If someone dies in a factory it's me or one of my colleagues and a notebook – if you're lucky.'

'Like Brightside Foundry.'

'Like Brightside Foundry – just me, a tape measure and the mighty sophistication of a twelve year old compact camera.'

I pulled my jacket round me as the evening air started to bite. 'So what happened at the Southwark site?'

'We don't exactly know. The police aren't even treating it as suspicious. They say there's nothing unusual about a forty-something single man deciding to go AWOL: midlife crisis they say. We don't buy that though. There's something very troubling. They haven't even checked CCTV so far as we know. We've been trying to get onto the site but haven't succeeded – they seem to be hand-picking labour really carefully, and we've not got into their computer system to work out which contractors they're bringing in next: the firewall is sophisticated. We've placed some lads working for contractors who are involved at the same site already, but those lads can't get onto the MacFarlane job. I was wondering if you knew the inspector that covers the side, Rhona Morgan? We know she's a union member but that's all. What if we were to approach her?'

'I've heard the name, but I don't know her. I can find out, maybe.'

'Discreetly though, yeah?'

'Hundred percent. You can count on me.'

I wandered back via the pub for one last bank holiday weekend pint – and in a vague hope that Jade might be there – I felt in need of a little warmth. What the hell had happened these last few weeks?

The world had suddenly gone bloody mad – like something from a film, with assassinations going on. Who was that guy who got done with an umbrella – Georgi Markov – was it? And that Russian bloke with the polonium – Alexander wotsisname. Was it Josh who was deluded? He did come across as a bit of a zealot. Should I go to the police? But then there was Abdi, who was as genuine and as straightforward a bloke as they come. I went back over the fact of the two deaths – all the evidence pointed to the truth of what Josh said – and my whole life approach, and philosophy, was based on evidence: if I ignored that I might as well start believing in a divine creator, denying climate change, believing in ghosts, and psychics – and that the world wasn't round.

I made a call the next day to a mate of mine at the London office on his personal mobile – someone I've known from way back – when we started together in the job – on the same training courses all the way through. One or two odd things had happened of late to union reps in our department – disciplinaries, even a sacking for misconduct – nothing we could pinpoint or scream from the rooftops, and all this talk of Josh's had put the wind up me – best avoid using the network's phones.

'Hey, Mike. It's Mitch. Quick favour. What do you know about Rhona Morgan?'

'She's a good inspector. Has a good enforcement profile. Why?'

'I just need to know something – it's union stuff. Can she be trusted with sensitive union stuff?'

'Not sure what you mean, mate. She is a bit flakey – not one of my most reliable members – she worked the last strike day, for example.'

'A scab then?'

'That's one way of putting it. Puts herself first. Maybe a Lib Dem?'

'Okay, that's answered it. Ta, Mike. Family okay…'

That meant we couldn't approach her for any information or help – look at me: using "we" to bracket myself with Josh and Abdi. I went back into the main office and clicked on the inspection database to see if I could find the inspection records of the MacFarlane site. Sometimes the records are unreliable or the inspectors themselves are dilatory in not filling in what they've been up too, so it might not turn anything up. The easiest way was to check Rhona Morgan's case list. I was straight to it – MacFarlane construction, Borough High Street. She'd left a good account of the inspection history – she was clearly a good inspector: asbestos removal, demolition, clearance – it was all recorded. Liaison with the designer and main client – an inspection of preliminary ground-works, dates for when the piling was started and concrete shuttering for the building. Various key documents were attached to the record that she must have scanned in: asbestos clearance certificates, method statements etc. Very thorough. She had planned in a return visit for four weeks' time when the steel erectors and craneage were due on site.

NINE

The day after our mock-kidnapping we all had one-to-ones with the person who was to be our handler; mine went by the name Raife. He had tutored on some of the courses on the international scene: European networks – most of which were to be avoided like the plague – groupings of fruit-and-nut jobs – morons like Anders Breivik. But there were some groups in Germany, Italy and the Netherlands in particular who were as well organised and disciplined as ours. We also had strong links in the United States. When I found out Raife was to be my handler I was really excited – trips to Florence and New York were on the cards. I had visions of wafting around Tuscany in loose fitting frocks or hitting Fifth Avenue with Daddy's credit card, or secret meetings with key people in Trump Towers.

I knocked and entered one of the large rooms on the first floor – bookshelves on the walls, a leather-topped desk by the window and thick, quality woollen carpet on the floor. Raife was sat on a classic red leather chesterfield with a glass coffee table in front of it with what looked like a Regency silver coffee pot and china cups set out on a tray.

'Coffee? It's Kopi Luwak – rather expensive – improved by passing through the intestinal tract of some sort of Indonesian weasel-thing apparently. You should try it.'

'No thanks. I'll pass.'

'I hear you performed rather well last night?'

'I've still not got over it.'

'Well you look serene, in spite of your adventure. None the worse for it. We have to do these things, I'm afraid – not just as a test, but for your own benefit – you will face some tough challenges and you will draw strength from all your time here.'

'Thanks. I'm really pleased to be working with you.'

'Good. We're trusting you with some work of the utmost importance. You're one of our best pupils, Kate.' I was now confident he would be sending me to Washington, or somewhere similar.

'You're going to Rawmarsh.'

At first the words did not compute – was it the name of a laboratory in somewhere like Geneva – the Rawmarsh Institute? or some think-tank, linked to an Ivy League University? I nodded as if I understood.

'It's near Rotherham' – I racked my brains. Did he mean Rotherhithe? – 'In South Yorkshire.'

I felt like the floor had given way and I was falling, my stomach feeling like I was in one of those super-fast lifts in tall buildings. I had been to Yorkshire once – to Harrogate. I'd heard friends scoffing at the thought of a Harvey Nicks in Leeds, but *South* Yorkshire? I'd rather be posted to the Yemen – wearing nothing but a bikini, decorated with Danish cartoons of a man in a turban. Raife smiled at me.

'You're kidding right? Nice one, you had me going there for a while.'

'I'm serious, Kate. We're posting you to the heart of the constituency of James Philpott. You'll be doing vital work there to save this nation from ruin. Of course we recognise that the Conservative Party has no chance whatsoever in influencing the vote there, but given a fair wind, Philpott could be unseated by UKIP – it just goes to show how naive voters can be in thinking that a party like UKIP is in touch with ordinary people. But that's the Great British electorate for you: just appeal to their base instincts, which of course is all that such feeble people have – nothing that can be equated with intellect. Just toss them a biscuit and they bark.

'It presents an excellent opportunity to completely run Philpott's little bandwagon into the nearest ditch. If it wasn't so important we wouldn't we putting our best man on the job, so to speak.'

'What would I be doing?'

'You'll be working with UKIP to strengthen their organisation and to inject wads of cash into the campaign under the radar. We will be working with lots of allies in the local press and in the BBC to gain maximum exposure for the campaign as it builds momentum, but we need to keep the UKIP swivel-eyed loons quiet, which will be a key part of your job. We also need to neuter one or two local individuals who are having a significant impact on motivating support for Philpott – there is a lot at stake here. It will involve one or two special jobs, unfortunate but necessary. You will stay invisible to the public – the story will never shift to you, your work is entirely in the shadows, under the wire etc, to use the vernacular. We have a candidate lined up – the first task is to get her in the post instead of the raving mad, coarse individual they always seem to fall back on – their local woman – she has some support amongst UKIP members but could never beat Philpott. We'll take care of the candidate selection at a national level, but you'll do all the groundwork at a local level. Our preferred candidate could wipe the floor with Philpott providing we can mobilize the foul individuals who are drawn to UKIP – the bigoted net curtain twitchers, idle epsilons who think hard-working people – or even those feckless, indolent white unemployed scumbags – are owed something, football thugs who blame immigrants for everything, people who park their cars on their concreted-over front gardens, and puffed up idiots who still idolise the grocer's daughter for selling them their council houses for the price of a decent case or two of Bordeaux.'

'You mentioned special jobs?'

'Don't worry, Kate. We're not asking you to do anything messy. It will be all carefully worked out so there is absolutely nothing for you to do but set in chain a sequence of events. We share that responsibility. Every day we make decisions for the greater good that we know will consign some unfortunate people to history – this is no different. When the Chancellor refuses to increase the budget to the NHS, and doctors get all uppity and start bleating about the consequences if certain drugs aren't properly funded, or when we decide not to spend billions on road safety we know that will have consequences in terms of collateral damage, but we take a societal view. There are people who specialise in assigning a cost to preserving an individual's life – and if it comes to more than a million pounds or so the investment is not considered worthwhile. If a drug costs more than fifteen thousand a year it probably isn't worth it just to keep someone alive. The National Institute for Health and Care Excellence set it a little higher for purely political reasons. That's just how it is. And of course we are dealing largely with insignificant lives here – all very tragic for the close family, of course, but, beyond that, does anyone really give an S-H-one-T?'

This was nerve-racking stuff, but I was also excited about having such an important role in history. So, I might never make it into the history books like Guillaume Fawkes or Lee Harvey Oswald, though they are bad examples in a way because they have been judged by history as being the baddies. Have you ever noticed how the ones on *our* side never get mentioned, never mind vilified? That's because we write the history books of course. Ha! We decide what goes in them – which version to tell the masses.

After seeing Raife, I went to receive my various identities, each with accompanying bankcards, drivers' licences etcetera, and was briefed on my backstories, which I was tested on in the following days.

I was kitted out with a rather tacky piece of luggage which I was told had been purchased from somewhere called "Wilkinson's" rather than Louis Vuitton, and I was given a new wardrobe to go in it – apparently only partially new, some of it being second-hand – lie back and think of England, Kate! Clothes that might actually have been worn by a shop-girl previously! For authenticity, they said. I had to do some studying on the locality, though fortunately my back-story saved me from having to immerse myself too deeply in the study of Rotherham "culture." I was from Grantham if anyone asked – these things amuse the brains which draw them up. "Oh, I'm new to Rawmarsh. *Cash Converters*? No, we don't have one of those in Grantham."

I was given my gadgets – button cameras, bugs, listening devices – I especially liked the one that can pick up vibrations on panes of glass using lasers and translate that into speech if anyone were talking in the room beyond that glass.

We were all allowed to return home for the weekend before being assigned, so I went back to Berkshire where the old man and his wife live. Spent some quality time with my favourite members of the family: Hermione and Leontes – my horses. I rode Leo for miles across the beautiful countryside around my home and felt the hand of history on me, so proud of this ancient land, and, as I cantered over rolling hills, I steeled myself for the battle ahead, for facing this new Armada, my generation's Waterloo, our finest hour.

I was dropped off by Raife at Luton Parkway station on the Monday, and had to run the gauntlet of some vile specimens waving homemade banners about their latest pathetic whinge — the politics of envy — wanting more money from hard-pressed taxpayers for their menial cleaning jobs or something. Well they should have paid more attention in school then shouldn't they?

By the time I had travelled on the disgusting little train full of epsilons from Sheffield to Rotherham, and sat in the back of a nasty taxi to my new digs in Rawmarsh, I was ready for a shower. The pathetic little trickle emerging from the yellowing plastic shower head was more like being squirted with a water-pistol from a cheap Christmas cracker.

It's amazing how much you can train your brain to accept once you get into a routine. I substituted Park Lane for Parkgate, Manolo Blahniks for white boots from Primark, Dior for Savacentre, Pret-a-Manger for Greggs, and Covent Garden for Mecca Bingo — just to get in with the right crowd. I bought a horrible little car on hire purchase and gave people lifts home. I signed on as a temp in an agency that was recommended by Raife and got a part-time job in a place packing electrical equipment. Anyone looking on from the outside would say I settled in quickly. I was soon gossiping along with the rest of the girls in the factory and singing along to tunes on Kiss FM. My "boyfriend," Connor (aka Raife), visited me every now and then — he worked away on the rigs, and had to live out of a caravan in Aberdeen for us to make ends meet — and we were saving up for our wedding: big dress and a honeymoon in Cancun — well you have to do it in style don't you?

I started weaving threads and manipulating people, spreading rumours about the sitting candidate and singing the praises for the new pretender Rosemary Haig — I was a dogged defender of British jobs for British people and denounced the influx of Slovakians and Poles — as bad as I'd seen it back in Lincolnshire. When the local rag reported my rumours afterwards, I became some sort of guru — like I could predict the future. I was invited into people's homes, and asked advice on all sorts of things, but I was always self-effacing and remembered to leave the glory to Rosemary. It was going to be a shoo-in. The old candidate came out fighting, but just made herself look bitter and vindictive. I then did some digging and found she had a link to a taxi firm that had been involved in ferrying underage girls to sex parties. Such gossip was of course dynamite in Rotherham. The link was really very tenuous – it was owned by a brother-in-law, and the girls might not actually have been underage – but by the time I had spun the story, the impression was that she was practically being accused of sex-trafficking herself. And, of course, the local rag, with some help from Raife and his contacts, reported the rumours, not so as to be libellous – they just said something like "it was wrong to make such allegations against a well-known local figure," but that very reporting made them sticky, and then the local news showed her in a late night, Baileys-induced, foul-mouthed tirade of abuse against muslims and communists who were conspiring against her. This made your average "respectable" UKIP supporter, who just feels that "things are not what they used to be," a little uneasy. The more she was cornered the more she clawed and spat until she was quietly removed and Rosemary installed in a new high street pop-up UKIP shop – over the road from some community kitchen's naive bid to wean the locals off chips and fizzy pop and onto salad and quinoa.

I had by this time been gathering intelligence on Philpott and his organisation, working with a local Labour Party member – one of ours – who was right there in the thick of it: recording, leaking, and briefing Perceval Society HQ. In particular I'd been observing the routine of a loud-mouthed union member who was proving to be a total pain in the arse. He was out on doorsteps in all weathers and, according to our insider, getting huge numbers of pledges of votes. It was not just him though, he was influential with the local Trades Council – where all these reds get together and plot, and was involved in training young party members in the key messages to get across on the door steps. I went to see him speak at an anti-EDL rally in town one Saturday, and you couldn't deny the man had charisma and a certain rough attractiveness. He clearly engaged his audience. He wasn't just an old-fashioned trade unionist, though.

He was astute on social media campaigns – @Yates_Prole was his
Twitter handle and he had over two hundred thousand followers, all
of them apparently genuine. He ran a popular blog called
"Reclaiming the State" – as if it was ever theirs. He also sang in a
band, and was something of a local celebrity. He was like some
gritty, authentic version of Owen Jones. This man clearly glorified in
his working class credentials, even seemed to feign pride in working
in a scruffy foundry – taking masochistic pleasure from being badly
treated. The chap clearly had something about him, so it was
beyond me why he had no aspiration to do something other than
melt down scrap aluminium. What Alan Duncan would have
described as a "low achiever."

I was reassigned by the agency to the foundry he worked in and
set about researching him. At first I read the briefings sent to me –
the guy was apparently genuine – not some inverted snob from
university pretending to be "down" with the working classes. He
was the son of a miner, pulled himself up by his bootstraps and got
his education through a trade union route.

I had never imagined that such places as that foundry existed in
the 21st century – the shed where the furnaces were was like
something from one of those mediaeval freezes depicting hell – fire,
choking smoke, heat, and nasty little servants of the devil moving
backwards and forwards pitchforking bodies into the flames – no,
sorry that last bit was just my imagination – they were lowering
aluminium scrap into oil-fired furnaces.

I worked hard whilst I was there and I overhauled their materials
handling system and brought it up to date – probably saved them
millions. My overall contribution to the business was definitely on
the side of credit not debit. The odious wide-boy in charge begged
me to stay on afterwards. He was desperate to get inside my
knickers. The very thought was enough to make me want to vomit.

It was quite an easy matter to work out, on a certain shift at a
certain time, which pallet of aluminium ingots was to be charged. I
simply slipped one under my coat when I was out with my clipboard
checking stock flows. Raife took it away and brought it back in time
for me to place it back in the destination pallet. I was amazed how
good a job had been done with it. You could hardly see the marks

where the solid block of aluminium had been drilled and sealed back up. It was an unfortunate industrial accident, compounded by the fact that the personal protective equipment wasn't flame retardant. What a tragic alignment of the stars. Hard to believe that such a thing could happen.

My next job was a postman. Normally, I quite like postman – comes from watching Postman Pat as a child, I guess. They are associated in my mind with nice things arriving in the post – little tokens of affection from my various admirers, or cheques from Daddy. But this one was different – he was wearisome in his devotion to his pathetic little beliefs. He rushed his postal round so that he could get back to doing his rabble-rousing – he was always popping up as the political agent for local councils and parliamentary seats for the reds, organising mass meetings and marches, lobbies of parliament, and cosying up to Billy Bragg and the likes. He was very effective, and very dangerous. He was so obviously a communist – talk of reds under the beds these types were in the bed, shagging the Labour Party up, down and sideways. God only knows how they had been allowed to creep back from political oblivion – did they learn nothing from the Militant years? – *What shall we call ourselves? - Militant, Geoff – what's wrong with that? – Get real, we need a new name – Something else beginning with M? – What about Momentum? – Sounds very happening. Nice one, Bob.* These people have no belief whatsoever in free markets, and advocated ridiculous notions like the removal of limited liability from all companies. How would you get entrepreneurs to take risks if they had to take personal responsibility should anything go wrong? We'd still be in mediaeval times. This Antichrist Postman Pat spent so much time on his little hobby that he never lifted a finger to clean his house – if he spent half so much effort on trying to make a bit of money he might have been able to employ a cleaner like normal people.

It was a much easier job than anticipated due to the general sloppiness of the man – the flue pipe to his new boiler worked free quite easily because it hadn't been finished well. I wasn't sure if it had worked at first – a bit hit and miss I thought, so the report in the local rag a week or so later was quite satisfying.

There was an angle I'd not covered though – it hadn't occurred to me that because it was a new boiler there was a possibility of some moron at the Health and Safety Executive sniffing round and asking questions of the person who installed the boiler. Anything other than an accidental death verdict would have created the wrong sort of publicity, so the police were asked to arrange it that the CPS wouldn't look into it, and to wipe the flue of the installer's prints just in case.

I thought that was that for a while. Things in the constituency were under control again, leaving Philpott a stiff climb to even retain his own seat, given our resurgent UKIP candidate and all the anti-immigration fervour that just needed an occasional stir every now and then. However, a small problem arose. It could have just been a coincidence, but I was informed that the inspector who had been asking awkward questions about my unfortunate deceased Postman Pat was going back over the Brightside Foundry job. We like to maintain "hygiene" after jobs to make sure there is no detectable footprint from our work – so we like to know of anything out of the ordinary. As a precaution I made some enquiries into this inspector.

TEN

I sat out in the Peace Gardens during my dinnertime break. The sun had brought out the office workers and shoppers and one or two small kids were in the fountain, in their pants, waiting for the foot-high spouts of water to shoot up and engulf them and their giggles.

I finished my pasty and leaned back on the bench to turn my face full on to the warmth of the sun, but, instead of relaxing, thoughts whizzed round the inside of my head and a bubbling anger refused to be quelled. Everyone sitting here on the grass, or stuffing their faces, or taking comfort from their purchases – heading sheep-like into a dangerous future and seemingly not bothered about their freedoms, or concepts like equality or justice. Bastards that voted in the referendum with bile in their throats and hate in their hearts. No, that wasn't fair – perhaps some of these people were like that, but Sheffield had not elected a Tory for decades – unless you counted Nick Clegg. Some of these people might be those that stopped their shopping to clap as we passed by with our banners back in March. No one really gave a stuff what these people thought – never had. It was a few hundred thousand votes in Middle England that counted, no one else mattered: if you weren't in a marginal seat no one in Westminster gave a shit. Almost as bad as the days of the rotten boroughs.

I tapped out a text for Abdi. 'Got some info.'

As I headed back to the office the phone buzzed: 'What time you finish work? I'll give you a lift.'

'5:15 – I'll wait down the side road. Ta.'

The black City Cabs car was parked up when I emerged from the building and turned down the side road. I got in the front seat.

'Good to see you, mate. How you doing?'

'Good. Thanks for this.'

We pulled away towards the ring road, the reporter on *PM* discussing the latest deaths of migrants in the Mediterranean off the coast of Libya. Another dodgy boat overloaded with desperate people, ripped off by human traffickers.

'I've been doing some research into that construction site in London, the one Josh was on about.'

'Yeah, he told me. Anything useful?'

'Not really. We can't use the inspector there though.'

'Pity.'

The traffic was bad as usual on St Mary's Gate. Abdi wound the window down and turned the radio up to compensate for the noise of the traffic. "*Some breaking news. We are getting unconfirmed reports of a shooting in Belgravia. It is believed that the target was the trade minister George Vernon-Harcourt.*"

Abdi slapped the steering wheel.

"*We'll bring you more news as we get it. London has been on the highest level of security, ranked as critical, following threats from Islamic extremists, but there is no indication of whether this is linked.*"

'This is big. It's started.' Abdi's voice was excited.

'What do you mean?'

'It's not Al Qaeda or ISIS.'

'You mean… was he Target Number One?'

Abdi turned to me and smiled. 'I don't know for certain, I'm not in the loop, but I expect so. The man was a nasty piece of work. Maybe this will make them realise they can't just do what they like. That was for Dave and Jon… and the others.'

We went up Bramall Lane and on to London Road in silence, waiting for more news on the radio.

We pulled up on my road as the chimes of Big Ben sounded for the six o'clock news. It was confirmed that it was Vernon-Harcourt, and that he had been shot dead by a single sniper bullet. The security correspondent was speculating whether this meant that Islamist terrorists had moved to a new level of sophistication and whether this meant that US military training for Syrian rebels had been misdirected.

"*This kind of targeted killing from a nearby rooftop or building involves hardware and training not previously seen out of NATO, Russia or China. The other possibility is that his links with Unionist groups in Northern Ireland has made him the target of dissident IRA groups, although again this does not follow their previous M.O. Now onto today's other news…*"

'This means things will hot up for a while.'

'Who for?'

'Possibly for all of us.'

'You got time for a cuppa?'

'Okay, ta.'

He went to the car boot and took out a rucksack. 'It would be a useful precaution in the circumstances to give it a quick scan.'

I went in and dumped my own bag on the table and went to fill the kettle while Abdi took out the scanner.

'You had anything to eat yet? I could rustle up some pasta or something?'

There was no reply. I looked up. Abdi was focused on the machine.

'No thanks,' he said. 'Change of plan. Let's go and get a takeaway.'

'What?'

He held up a finger to his lips and headed for the door. I followed. He went straight to the car and got in.

'What's going on?' I said, as I sat down next to him.

'I found something.'

'What?'

'A bug of some sort.'

'No way. In my house? Can you get it out?'

'Yes, but if we do they'll know we're onto them. Better leaving it there. Go and lock up, we'll go and see what Josh reckons.'

I was shaking with anger and fear now. How on earth had they got into my house? Someone must have been in. But I'd seen no signs of a break in. I picked up my phone, keys and bag off the table, turned to leave, then went back in and pulled out a bottle of Wyborowa vodka from the cupboard and locked up.

'What sort of bug, Abdi?' I said as we headed across town to his house.

'It could be anything – listening device, could be cameras too. We have to assume the worst. They may have accessed your computer.'

'I mostly use my phone now.'

'On roaming or through your wi-fi?'

'Both.'

He sucked his teeth.

'But how did they get in, and why me?'

'Getting in is not difficult in most houses, though your doors and windows are pretty good. I don't know. It must be that they've got wind of the work you've been doing. That means they're rattled. It's a good sign.'

'Good? Someone's been in my bloody house! What have you got me into here?'

'Don't worry, Mitch. It will be all right. You're small-fry, just a source of information.'

'Thanks for that.'

I sulked for the rest of the journey.

Abdi's house in Shiregreen was unremarkable: a small terraced house just off a busy road. We went in through the front door, straight into the front room with a settee and TV.

'Come in, sit down. I'll be with you in a minute.'

He went through to the room at the back, the house being one of those divided by the staircase. I put the telly on and caught the tail end of the local news. I say "local," but it's always about Leeds really, and ignores Sheffield. Total cultural hegemony – even so far as effacing our identity. It is "Leeds swimmer" this, or "Leeds singer" that, whereas Joe Root is not "Sheffield cricketer" but "Yorkshire cricketer," Danny Willett is a "Yorkshire golfer." The presenters talk about "we," meaning Leeds and grin when announcing Leeds United results and are deadpan when it comes to the South Yorkshire ones.

'I've spoken to Josh. We reckon you're best not going back tonight just in case. He's going to come round in a bit. Can I get you owt?'

'You got any beer?'

'No, sorry. Mango juice? Tea?'

'Any ice?' I got the bottle out of my bag. 'Medicinal. Bring a glass for yourself too.'

He brought two glasses with ice in.

'I thought you didn't drink.'

'I said I'm not supposed to.' He smiled and knocked back the vodka.

'It's better when the bottle's straight from the freezer, without the ice watering it down, but this is not bad.'

'Josh is bringing food too.'

While we waited I checked my e-mails on my work phone. I had sent an e-mail to an engineering works, asking if I could switch my next day's visit to nine o'clock in the morning since I'd had to cancel another inspection. I wanted to check if it was okay. There was also an email from my boss saying: "Please report to the office in the morning. I need to see you about something important. I have arranged for Jim O'Neill to be there too." I had no idea what this meant, but it was most unusual. Jim O'Neill was an inspector who dealt with chemical works. "Report to the office" was a peculiar turn of phrase. Not: "can you call into the office," or "I have arranged a meeting."

We got sat around the table in the kitchen with the tin foil curry containers and a bag of roti that Abdi tipped into a pile on a plate.

'You want a knife and fork?'

'Yes please. I've tried without, but always make a mess. There's a knack to it.'

Josh had brought some cans of beer, too. 'Curry and beer – cross-cultural perfection,' he said.

'So what am I to do?' I said.

'I think you'd best not go home until we've figured it out. If you don't know what to do – haven't been trained in how to deal with it, it is hard to act natural and not give the game away – as soon as you start wondering where the bugs are and go looking for them, they'll know they're rumbled – better to keep them thinking. It's very hard not to go looking about – especially if there are cameras installed – they'll spot you.'

'Cameras?'

'You'd be amazed how easily a camera with a transmitter can be concealed. They could have swapped your phone charger for one with a camera, or your smoke alarms.'

'Yeah, okay. That's freaking me out. I'd rather not be there.'

'They're only after information, I suspect – not you. Someone knows you've been asking questions, I presume.'

I put down my knife and fork. 'Shit! That could be what my boss wants to see me for.' I explained the "report to the office" e-mail. 'I've had an idea though.'

After tea, I got my laptop out and logged in whilst Abdi tidied up and me and Josh sat on the settee.

At Easter, I deputised for my boss for two weeks while she went scuba diving in the Caribbean with her perfect family. I noticed the other week that she had forgotten to disable my access to her e-mail inbox. I'd resisted the temptation to go snooping around it because she'd probably find out. I should have just told her, but instead I thought: "sod her, why should I?"

My heart was racing and my armpits dampened my shirt as I typed her name into the "open other folder" box. Perhaps she'd noticed and disabled it. I clicked "ok," and watched the screen blink and open in her inbox. I scanned the list for anything interesting. There were the usual updates on what was happening at management levels, circulars about lifts not working etcetera. She was one of those awful people who only have emails in their inbox that are less than a week old, whereas ordinary mortals leave them there until the system deletes them automatically. But no, Patricia deals with things, then efficiently deletes or files them. There was also an unopened message from her boss marked "staff in confidence – to be opened by addressee only." I hovered the cursor over it and clicked. I skimmed through the message and I got a feeling in my stomach like I was in a construction hoist climbing the side of a tower block. "I tried contacting you on your mobile but remembered you said you were out tonight at the Hallé, hence this email so that you get the message before your disciplinary in the morning. I have just come off the phone with the chief executive, and he wants this nipping in the bud – he is under pressure from above, given events. Of course you will deal with it by the book, but the outcome is not in doubt, Roger."

'Shit! Shit! Shit!' The reason for Jim O'Neill's presence at the meeting tomorrow was clear. He was the union rep – she was playing it by the book so as to give me no chance to put in a grievance. Playing it by the book and throwing that book at me.

'What's up, Mitch?'

'You'd better look at this, quick. I need to come off it before they realise I'm on the network.'

He read it; then I clicked "mark unopened" on the message and logged off.

'What have you done, Mitch?'

'Nothing. That's the point. Don't you see that it can only be me accessing the MacFarlane records. It's against the rules to access stuff you're not working on – people do it all the time though out of curiosity – when it's so easy to have a peek at stuff in the news, like the inside view on an Alton Towers investigation, or something else in the news, some find it hard to resist – but this is heavy beyond belief if that is it.'

'Could it be anything else?'

'No. I'm squeaky clean me. It must be a fit up – you saw what it said: given recent events or something, wasn't it? What else can it mean? Other than a reference to the assassination?'

'It's a bit of a leap, but… I dunno.'

'Think about it. How else would they know I'd looked at those records this morning unless they'd been keeping a close eye on me? They've been waiting for me to put a foot out of line. They're going to suspend me until they can dig around for enough other stuff to trump something up. This is your bloody fault! There must be a link between your target number one, this journalist disappearing, and the information I've passed to you, otherwise why would I being hung out to dry like this? For fuck's sake! There's no way I'm going in in the morning. Pass me that bottle.'

I woke up the next day feeling like death warmed up. I looked around for my radio alarm clock to tell me the time but it wasn't there. I then realised I wasn't in my room at all. I was in a strange bed in a room with chocolate brown curtains. I remembered being in Abdi's house but not going to bed. That e-mail. I groaned and sat up – I was just wearing my boxers. I found my clothes folded on a wooden chair and found my watch in my pocket. Twelve-thirty. I got dressed and staggered downstairs. Someone was sat at the kitchen table – a man in his early twenties.

'Good morning – or is it afternoon? I'm Shaf, Abdi's cousin. You sleep okay? Abdi said you been drowning your sorrows last night. I'll just get him.' He spoke down his phone. 'Your mate – back in land of living. Okay, see you. He is coming back – help yourself to breakfast. Fridge there. Kettle there. There's clean towel for you on the side of the bath too.'

I found the remains of a carton of mango juice and put the kettle on. I got a shower and was sitting on the settee with a second mug of tea when Abdi came in the front door.

'Cheers, Shaf. Here's the keys. I'll ring you later. How's it going, mate? Any better?'

'Yeah. Fair to shite.'

'You were a bit worse for wear last night. You shouldn't drink that stuff if you can't take it.'

'Sorry, Abdi. I don't remember much.'

'No, I had to put you to bed and get you undressed. You could barely move unaided. You slept like a log though.'

'You mean we shared a bed?'

'Well, I wasn't going to sleep on this old settee was I? Not when I had to be up at half four. Don't worry I didn't take advantage of you or nothing.'

'How do you mean? Oh… I hadn't realised.' I paused. 'I might not have minded.'

He laughed at me. 'Some other time, maybe.'

'Seriously though – I'm sorry to put you to any trouble.'

'No trouble. We've got you in this, so it is the least we can do. I'm just going to grab a sandwich for lunch, then get some kip. Did you want anything?'

'No. Ta. I just had breakfast.'

'You're welcome to stay here until we work out what to do with you – make yourself at home.'

I sat with my eyes closed. I'd found paracetamol in the bathroom cabinet and my head was feeling a little better now, but I was in no fit state to go into work, besides I didn't fancy facing the music, or

the lovely Patricia. I checked my work phone – there was a
voicemail from her saying she was disappointed I'd neither come to
work nor phoned in if I was ill, and an e-mail from her rearranging
the meeting for the following morning. I replied to the e-mail saying
I thought I had food poisoning from a curry and that I hoped to be
in in the morning. It is always less convincing claiming food
poisoning as a vegan: no raw chicken, no dodgy prawns, no bad
shellfish to blame – tofu being less infamous in this area. I had not
been in a fit state to get to my phone until now, I said. Terribly sorry
– blah, blah.

I went to the local shops and bought a paper and some Liquorice
Allsorts – just the thing for a hangover I find. There weren't many
details of the Vernon-Harcourt shooting – a picture of the scene in
London and an ambulance, and a load of speculation, little more,
but I suppose it had only happened a few hours before they went to
press. The BBC News Channel hadn't been much more
enlightening – not much "news" at all in fact, just more wheeling
out of so-called experts to speculate and blather. When did this
trend for waffle rather than facts start? Froth not substance. I
bought some apples and plums to make a crumble with, and some
tomatoes for soup. At least I could make myself useful whilst
imposing on someone's hospitality.

I dozed a bit myself in the afternoon on the settee whilst
watching Countdown.

Abdi washed up after tea, and I grabbed a tea towel to wipe.

'Listen, I've been thinking – I'm in this now. I can't go into work
as things stand. So, in for a penny, in for a pound. Why don't I go
and see what I can find out about this MacFarlane job? I could use
my position to get onto the site and have a look round. It'd be a
doddle. What would be the best information I could gather?'

'I don't know if we should expose you to any more risk.'

'Well it might not be your call. I might go anyway, whether you
approve or not. I just need to go back to the house for a few things.
My hi-vis and hard hat, and a rucksack and change of clothes.'

'I dunno, Mitch.'

'Look, Abdi. I've thought it through. I've no job left. I can't go in my house. I'm not staying here watching daytime telly when I can help you beat these guys. Josh said you can't find a way onto the site, and you want to know what happened to that journalist, don't you? And, if he was bumped off, who did it? Target One's out of the way. I've given you a Target Two. Who else you got? They've made this personal now.'

'Okay. I'm seeing Josh later. I'll see what he thinks.'

I woke the next morning to Asian Dub music coming from the kitchen. I dressed and went down. Abdi was frying eggs.

'Shall I put you one on?'

'I don't eat eggs. Neatly encapsulated chicken periods, them.'

'You're weird you are. I keep forgetting just how weird. Help yourself to whatever rabbit food you can find.'

'Ta.' I filled the kettle. 'What time did you get back? I didn't hear you?'

'No, I stayed out. Not been back long.'

'What did you decide? You know, about this MacFarlane site?'

'He says to go for it, if you're sure.'

'Yes, I am.'

'When will you go?'

'As soon as I can get my stuff.'

'I'll get Shaf to take you round.'

He phoned his cousin. 'Got a job for you, cuz. From here, yeah. Okay, laters. He is on an airport job, but he'll be back around midday.'

He then ran up the stairs and returned with an envelope. 'It won't be safe for you to use your bankcard – if they are on to you they'll have an alert on your card – or will once they realise you've done a runner. Best speak to your boss and tell her you'll go in.'

'I've already e-mailed her yesterday. She thinks I'm going in today.'

'Good. There's five hundred in cash in there. If you give me your bankcard and PIN we'll use it to make it look like you're still around. Also it's probably best not to use your mobile, except for the one I gave you. They could also monitor your mother's phone, for example, to see who phones her, then trace the caller on GPS.'

'Can they do that? Sounds more like something off the telly.'

'Except this is for real. Where have you told your boss you are? At home?'

'No, I've not said.'

'Let's keep it that way.'

I gave Abdi a man hug when he headed up to bed and waited for Shaf's return.

When we got to Woodseats, I went in the house without the usual feeling of returning to my base, my place of safety, my sanctuary from the world outside. Now the very worst of that "outside" was right here in the house. I got my rucksack from the back of the wardrobe and stuffed in a couple of pairs of socks and pants, my jeans and a shirt and trainers. I was still in the clothes I wear for work and my smart shoes from the day before. I chucked in a toothbrush and a deodorant, my hair putty and my iPod. That would do. I locked the door behind me, resisting the urge to shout something abusive to anyone that might be listening in on the bugs, wherever they might be.

I then got my personal protective equipment out of the car: my hi-vis, boots and hard hat, then put the rucksack on the back seat of Shaf's and Abdi's car.

'You ready?'

'Yes. Good. We need to go. We might have trouble.'

'How do you mean?'

'There's a black Toyota – don't look round – parked up the road. They seem interested in what's going on. Could just be a couple of blokes on their lunch break, but we soon find out. Where we going now?'

'To Midland Station, please.'

'I'll go interesting route – see if they're still with us. They've set off behind us. Can I ask you just to look ahead – not turn round, we don't want them to know that we know yet.'

He headed up round the back, past the top end of Meersbrook Park and down through Heeley.

'When I turn next corner I want you to get down so they don't know you are still in car, okay?'

My heart was now racing, and I was having very serious regrets. Perhaps going in to see Patricia, playing the innocent dupe and pleading for my job was a better option.

I could now only guess where we were from the view I had crouching uncomfortably in the foot-well.

'I'm going to try and lose them in traffic on Queen's Road.'

I could see the tops of buildings and gantry signs as we weaved between lanes. Then there was a screech of tyres and Shaf accelerated through the lights at the last minute and was racing up the hill.

'Right, I've got a plan. I'm cutting through All Saints School – you know it? Then out the back way onto Granville Road, so long as the gate's open. Then I want you to get out at the college – at traffic lights, and join the students at the tram stop. One stop along and you're right into the back of the station and cars can't go that way, yeah? I'll then head off hoping they'll follow me.'

Shaf sped up Norfolk Park Road and screeched round the corner into the school where the Goals 5-a-side football centre was. I knew it well.

'Can you get into the back now, while I'm driving.' He was going a bit slower as he weaved round through the school. I clambered over and got my rucksack on my back. On Granville Road he stopped at the lights at the bottom.

'Okay, quick, go! Good luck.'

I jumped out as fast as I could and ran to the tram stop where there was indeed a group of students milling about waiting for the tram into town. I got behind them just as I saw the black Toyota heading down towards the ring road. The tram came soon after, but it seemed like an age. The conductor hadn't made it as far as the back of the tram before we'd travelled the one stop. I ran into the station then was gripped with fear at going out onto the busy concourse at the front and being exposed when I bought a ticket. I looked down the length of the footbridge and saw two men just coming up the steps at the far end. I had no idea what the men pursuing us had looked like, but I ran straight down the first stairs

just in case and ran towards a train on platform 8 and got in just
before it pulled away. It was a Manchester train. This was not
exactly a direct route to London. I went up the other end from
where I'd seen the guard when I boarded; my first thought being to
try to get round not having a ticket. I slumped in a seat behind my
rucksack and pretended to sleep. The guard came into the carriage.

'Meadowhall and Sheffield tickets, please.' He went straight past
me – I had worked out my innocent story if he prodded me awake
about needing to be at the airport for a flight, and a sob story as to
why I'd not had time to queue at the station.

I got out at Stockport, checking the train as I got off to see who
got off with me, and then bought a ticket to Crewe.

At Crewe, I got off again and did the same checks before buying
a ticket to London. My logic was that this was harder for anyone to
work out where I was going if I was picked up on CCTV. I had also
changed on the train into my jeans and a hoodie, so that I could
keep my face hidden from cameras. Had I completely lost a grip on
reality? Almost certainly – I felt I had no idea what was going on,
nor where all this was heading, that I was just being rolled along by
fate. And the truth of it was the adrenaline rush was unlike anything
I'd ever known – in a weird way I was getting a thrill from being on
the set of a movie in which I was the star.

I was in London for about three thirty, not that much later than
if I'd gone direct and it had cost me less than forty quid. Okay, I had
dodged part of the fare, but still.

I bought a *Guardian* and a *Telegraph* at Euston to get two
perspectives, and went to find a hotel down on Gower Street –
small, cheap, but a clean bed. It seemed to be run by a Russian,
which seemed to fit in with the film I was featuring in.

It was warm in the little room so I lay on the bed in just my
pants and texted Abdi: 'Arrived. All good.' His message came back:
'Good. S told me about it. He says it worked. Go steady.'

The main story in the newspapers was still the shooting of
George Vernon-Harcourt. It was indeed a sniper from a nearby
building, they thought – there was speculation as to which one – the
papers explored possible motives – dissident Provisionals were the
favourites, perhaps having been involved with Eastern European

nationalists they had obtained what must have been a very sophisticated rifle, perhaps from Russian Crimea. It wasn't believed that there was any particular reason he would have been singled out by Islamist groups. The *Telegraph* ran a lengthy obituary – he was the son of a baron, his father was still occasionally wheeled out to vote in the Lords. The inheritance would now pass to his younger brother Theodore.

The *Guardian* ran a piece about his political views including repatriation of anyone with a criminal record, even if second generation, his strongly monarchistic views and his links with groups involved in something called *identitarianism*, which from what I could tell was an international grouping of neo-nazis and white supremacists. He had spoken on platforms with PEGIDA leaders and even with a leading light of the Tea Party movement with links to the Ku Klux Klan.

I found a little vegetarian curry house on a street down by Euston station and had an early night, ready for the following day's site "inspection."

Y ou stupid, stupid boy, Mitch. Why couldn't you just have done what you were supposed to? There was never any intention to do more than get you suspended for a while. Let you stew, make it clear that you had to fall in line and concentrate on your job of plodding round poor unsuspecting businesses making them sort out their risk assessments, clean their lavatories and wear their safety helmets and goggles – stop all this stupid dabbling in things you didn't understand, thinking you were being clever. But no, you had to be the maverick and not turn up to take the rap over your knuckles, run home to Mummy promising to be a good boy in the future and never do it again.

I now know that if I played it different – that if Jade had stuck around she would have tamed you, tied you to her with bonds of silk and gold thread, had you licking cream off the palm of her hand, jumping when she said jump, and coming running home to her every evening to whisper in her ear and snuggle up to her on your sofa. Oh you stupid boy.

I looked out through the glass windows separating those of us in the hotel from the great unwashed beyond: eating their pasties, with grubby fingers flicking phone screens, unruly children running up and down the paths between the palm trees and foliage.

I'd had a breakfast meeting with some contacts from the Chamber of Commerce and the Federation of Small Businesses about how to stage media coverage over the next few months. Preferring the calm of the hotel to the streets outside, I stayed behind to catch up on my e-mails and to reflect on the overall plan to leave Philpott floundering to catch up. One of his closest advisors was also passing us information about his plans so that if he'd tried to get on the front foot we could knock him straight back again. If he so much as stepped inside a hospital without using the hand-sanitizer, we'd make sure the story was about his filthy mitts on the ward rather than whatever clap-trap he'd wanted to spout about waiting lists.

The introduction to Purcell's *Cold Song* came through on my i-phone. The screen said: Connor.

'Hello Connor darling, how's Aberdeen and all those butch roughnecks?'

'Are you free to speak?'

'Yes, I'm fine, Raife, just bored.'

'Well, I've got something for you. Miller's gone AWOL. We need you to track him down. This character is proving a bit more awkward than we thought. We suspect he is now no longer working alone: perhaps he has closer ties than we first thought. Some sort of cleanskin. We'll let you know as soon as we have orders. But we need to find out what he's up to and locate him first. He is now to be treated as a potential target.'

I logged on to the Secure-net system and opened up Miller's file. I went to the live link to his house – it was quiet. I went to his personal email account, nothing there. His browser history: nothing on his home computer for a few days. Just some boring football stuff and iPlayer on his phone. His work e-mail showed some activity the previous day and an e-mail exchange with his manager saying he would be in work today. It was by then ten-thirty and there was no sign of him. No ATM transactions since Saturday and he last used his credit card on Monday at a garden centre in the Hope Valley. Come on Miller, where are you? I went to "play back" from his home. The last activity was on Tuesday evening at about six in the evening:

'You had anything to eat yet? I could rustle up some pasta or something?' – what a sweet boy. Then there was a pause:

'Er, no thanks. Change of plan. Let's go and get a takeaway.'

'What?'

And that was it. A bit odd, that. It could be nothing. Or could that pause be more significant?

I called for a driver, put on my hoodie and my shades and went to wait for the car outside.

We'd not been waiting an hour outside his house when Miller showed up in a silver taxi. He went in the house – all we could hear on the receiver was the banging of doors. Then he came back out a

few minutes later with a rucksack, and opened the boot of his car –
it looked like he was going on a trip. But instead he shut the boot
and still had the rucksack. I got ready to follow him on foot, but
then the same silver taxi came up the road and he got in.
Fortunately, we were parked facing the right way as it would have
been impossible to turn the car around on these stupidly narrow
streets, built for nothing more than the weekly dust cart and rag-
and-bone man or whatever it was. This turned out to be no ordinary
taxi though. My driver followed at a safe distance at first, then after
a few minutes said:
    'Why is he going this way?'
    'What do you mean?'
    'He's heading back to the main road again – you wouldn't come
this way – the speed bumps and priorities to oncoming vehicles –
and takes twice as long.'
    'Where have they gone?'
    'They're just ahead – but they must be on to us. Not even sure if
the target is still in the vehicle. Can you see him anywhere?'
    We were back on the main road and the taxi was now dodging in
and out of the lanes near a retail park and a big B&Q.
    'He must still be in the car unless this is a decoy.'
    Then they slowed right down, just a few cars ahead of us. There
were traffic lights ahead, which just changed to red as the taxi
veered off to the right. We were stuck.
    'You idiot! Get after them!'
    My driver had to manoeuvre round the stationary traffic in front,
and through the red light as horns started honking. Then he made a
dash when there was a gap in the oncoming traffic. The taxi was out
of sight. I stamped the foot-well.
    'Where's it gone?'
    'He's turned left up by the park, it's a one way road at the
bottom end – you look out for it parked up on the right hand side –
there's a school and sports field.'
    The driver put his foot down and took the speed bumps at over
sixty, sending my stomach bouncing up into my chest.
    'We've lost them.'

'No, keep going.' I checked the turn offs to the right, then a school came up on the left – just as we flew past I thought I saw a silver car at the far end of the car park.

'I think that was them round the back of the car park. Turn back.'

'Which way was he going?'

'Left.'

'There's a route through to another entrance which comes out on to the main road we join just at the top here. They might be doing that.'

'Go for it then.'

We joined the main road and turned left. It was busy road – but didn't take us long to get down it.

'I've seen them,' the driver said. 'Just going through the lights at the bottom.'

He raced on, just making it through before they changed. We were gaining on them now in the traffic and managed to get alongside at some lights on the dual carriageway. I looked across. The driver looked straight back at me and smiled, like I'd just given him an all-inclusive package trip to the Hajj. There was no one in the car with him. That wasn't the end of it. I was going to find out who owned that cab.

I spoke to Raife from the cafe at Waitrose – at least there was one small haven of semi-normality in this hellhole – while the driver waited outside as punishment.

'Not to worry,' Raife said. 'He has to turn up again soon. Where do you think he's gone?'

'I don't know. Could be anywhere.'

'No, people follow patterns of behaviour.'

'It wasn't far from either the bus station or the railway station when we lost him.'

'So where would he go?'

'He was sniffing around the records on the MacFarlane site. He could have gone to London.'

'I was wondering the same thing, but I trust your judgement better than mine. You know him. We still don't have any intelligence on Top Cat, but it just got a hell of a lot more interesting around here. We could do with finding out if he is after something.'

'Okay, Raife. I'll head to Town this afternoon.'

Staring out of the East Midland first class carriage gave me time to think. And they were not rational, analytical thoughts. The puzzle I was solving was not a dissection of the game-play of my target, how to close down on him, lock him in to moves I had planned several steps ahead. That was what I should have been doing, but my mind was wandering, and the puzzle I was coming back to was *why* I couldn't keep a focus? Part of me was looking forward to seeing Mitch again, just seeing the way he moved, the way he was at ease *dans son peau* as the French would say. He was happy in himself, his clothes didn't fit him – he fit them, if that makes sense. He could get away with wearing just about anything: he didn't try to look good, he just did. And yet there was a vulnerability about him.

So, what would be his next move? Assuming he was going to London, he'd need money so that would give him away – I'd check as soon as I got to the Lincoln's Inn office: see what his activity was. He'd get there no earlier than three o'clock. Not likely he'd go straight to the site, as he'd not get across to Southwark much before four. More likely he'd go there in the morning. And I'd be waiting for him. I'd not be able to let him see me of course, but I'd perhaps get to see his smile. Kate, Kate: this is ridiculous. A one-night stand, purely business that's all it was. And yet… He was the only boy I'd ever been with who didn't see me as a trophy, who didn't just take me for what he could get out of it – be that his own gratification or for the all-expenses-paid ride. Mitch wanted *me*, not just wanted to shag me and chalk me off on his bedpost. He'd got his pleasure from my pleasure; he smiled to see me smile. For the love of God, Kate!

I couldn't face a hotel room on my own so I looked up Will on my phone and sent him a message. Will wasn't exactly a boyfriend as such but he was a fairly regularly lay. Someone I went back to every now and then. He still held a flame for me. I met him at Matty Parker Street at some tiresome function or other. He was entertaining a small group of bright young things with his impersonations of John Redwood singing the Welsh national anthem. My God. How he ever came back from that humiliation – it shows the guts or is it just the chutzpah of those types. Most ordinary people would have done the decent thing and left their clothes on the beach and swum out to sea, or at least never shown their faces in public ever again.

Anyway, Will and I got talking and it turned out he had a flat with a balcony overlooking the river. His bedroom wall was glass, and from lying in bed you could see all the way down towards St Paul's and when privacy was required, at the flick of a switch, somehow the whole of the glass wall turns opaque. Then, when you woke in the morning, you could open your eyes to that view.

He had a plum job working for a German investment bank. In idle, drunken moments I had allowed myself to become entangled as he discussed his plans to move to a house in Surrey once he had made enough money to set himself up comfortably. He would have then just run a small operation from home, leaving him plenty of time to bring up a family and play golf several times a week.

'You would make a wonderful mother, and wife, Kate. You could be in charge of the house if you like – plan to do it however you liked: furnishings, pool, stables, whatever you fancy. We'd rub along just nicely, you and I.'

He is quite funny and charming is Will. Just not the sort to arouse any passion in a girl. He's safe. Predictable. Maybe that is just what I needed right then.

'Are you doing anything tonight?' my message read.

The train pulled into Leicester – can there be a place more bland – whoever goes to Leicester? Why? What on earth can all these people getting off have as a purpose?

A message came back. 'As it happens I was off to La Boheme tonight with Giles, but he knows which side his muffin is buttered on. So I'll meet you there at 6 and we'll have supper in the Amphitheatre. Rather that than the Crush – cold food for dinner, just so wrong.'

'You're such a sweetie, Will. xxx' I replied.

I started a mental list of all the boys and men that I had had. Could I say I had loved any of them? Love? How ridiculous – relationships were transactions – things of mutual benefit that last as long as those benefits were reciprocated. I would be entertained for an evening and dined in style and, in return, Will would get the best sex he had had since the last time he saw me.

But none of them had made me laugh quite so much as Mitch – I had mostly pitied them or felt my superiority, but not with Mitch. I had even felt secretly guilty for listening in on the bugs I'd hidden, but it had also given me a thrill, hearing him making his weekend plans with his cousin. Perhaps Jade could contrive to bump into him again? But that was just stupid.

He had not been self-conscious about his body. He hadn't strutted about – look at the product of all those hours of self-love at the gym – hadn't been shy – it was what it was for him, take it or leave it. But it was more than that – it was beautiful. Even his *thing* – and so often they're just ridiculous to look at, but not Mitch. Oh God, Kate!

Well perhaps the least I could do was make things easier for him – stop him becoming a live target. Perhaps warn him off. Say goodbye to him properly.

I needed to sort out some practicalities, so, on arrival at St Pancras I got a cab to a boutique in Covent Garden that specialises in vintage clothing. Now don't get me wrong, this is nothing like my objection to wearing a second-hand Top Shop skirt. I fancied something a bit more haute couture: a timeless classic black Dior number perhaps.

I tried various things on including a gorgeous multi-coloured Balestra gown. But at three grand plus, I questioned its practicability – for something I might just abandon at Will's flat. In the end I was a very good girl and settled for something cheap: a seventies Bill Blass black taffeta gown that was only about five hundred. Simple, classic. That also made the choice of heels an easy one. On the downside, probably because I was not exactly splashing out, or because I had turned up in jeans and a hoodie, the assistant had the nerve to suggest I might want to go looking for shoes myself in shops, rather than have them brought to me. It only took one of my looks for him to retract it: 'Or if you prefer I'll bring you some to try on.'

'Just get me some size six black D&Gs, nothing fancy… and some accessories. I'm paying *you* to decide what goes with the dress.'

They bagged up my "Sharon" clothes, and, after the application of a bit of lippy, I left in a cab as Kate again to the beautiful sound of swishing silk and compliments.

Will was waiting for me at the table in the restaurant with two champagne cocktails set out on the table. The darling had not even had a sip as he waited. He said all the appropriate things. I clearly boosted his self-esteem. And quite frankly he needed it. No matter how many thousands you spend on Harris Tweed at Savile Row, and no matter how modern or funky the design, it's still not quite the thing for the ROH in my opinion. Poor love. He needs a woman – desperately.

'Still waiting for me, Will?'

'As ever, Kate. Always waiting for you. Sit. You need to choose your main course – in the interests of being in our seats for curtain-up, I took the liberty of ordering you the venison carpaccio for starters. I'm afraid, though I am more than happy to wait for you, the curtain at the Opera won't.'

'Not even for me?'

'They should. But alas…'

A waiter hovered nearby.

'I'll have the lobster risotto then.'

'And I'll have the turbot please.'

He raised his glass. 'Here's to you, Kate. I don't know how you do it but you seem to get more beautiful every time I see you.'

'Okay, you can put that lolling tongue away and stop drooling now. You never know, I might just not have got around to looking for a hotel yet.'

He smiled as his mind raced on five or six hours. We ordered desserts for the interval then found our seats in the Grand Tier.

'Look, don't get all uppity with me, Kate. These seats were perfectly fine for me and Giles. Had you given me more notice I might have got you a box, but beggars can't be choosers.'

'I think you'll find it will be you doing the begging before the night is out, Will, darling.' I whispered in his ear. I enjoyed watching the colour rise in his neck. I kissed him on the cheek and sat down. 'I might even let you hold my hand.'

I must point out that Will is not someone to feel sorry for. This is the way he likes things: to be teased, though not in a cruel way. I keep him on a tight leash, metaphorically, and before the night's out he might even be on one, literally. He loves it – it's what he's used to. His gratification throughout his life, at home, at boarding school, and after, came from those temporary releases from his constraints. He needs rules and restrictions, and his anticipation of being able to break them builds noticeably the more you do it.

At first I thought the performance rather silly, and didn't relate much to the characters in their shabbiness, but once Mimi appeared I started to be drawn into the story. The scene as she falls in love with Rodolfo after their hands accidentally touch in the dark when looking for her key is undoubtedly beautiful.

There was something troubling me though, unsettling me as the story continued to unwind. There is something about live opera – the nakedness of the voices that creates a resonance inside you somewhere. Once, in Madeira, I was walking near the beach and I became aware of a curious sensation within me and strands of my hair started to drift skywards – there was static building in the air: presaging a storm and affecting my mood as well as my hair. Those operatic voices in the air somehow make something inside you vibrate, trigger responses in axons. I was relieved when the interval arrived accompanied by chocolate fondant, strong coffee, and idle chat.

The plot of Bohème, I have always thought to be rather ridiculous and had willed Mimi to go off and leave the loser that is Rodolpho behind, to find someone rich as he himself half hoped, so that she could get the medicine she needed. I always despised Rodolpho for not being firmer – you suspect he secretly gets a kick out of keeping her tied to him.

This time though something happened to me. As she lay dying in his arms complaining about her cold hands, I felt my nose tingle. *Qui… amor… sempre con te! Le mani… al caldo… e… domire.* I had to look away and think of something else to stop a stupid tear from ruining my mascara. I rested my head on Will's shoulder and reminded myself to collect my bags from the cloakroom, and thought I'd have to go and freshen up while he sorted out a cab.

Will brought out an expensive bottle of grappa when we got to his flat and some gorgeous handmade chocolates. He continued his forages into naughty-boy-territory, and eventually, and inevitably, he got what he was looking for.

He was asleep when I returned from the bathroom. I lay down. I was tired but sleep was some way off, so I put on Will's bathrobe and tiptoed across the beech-wood floor to the balcony and slid the door, almost silently, far enough to create a gap for me to slip through.

The city was beautiful – the night sky was clear and cool and lights shimmered in the river and stretched up into the sky blocking out all but the brightest stars. It wasn't quiet, but it was peaceful – like I was in a cocoon of stillness hovering above the city still active with people and transport.

Inside, Will slept contented, and somewhere out there, on his own, was Mitch.

A siren sounded some distance off – marking some tragedy in someone's life: perhaps a life drawn short. Will was the closest I'd had to a companion: someone I could contemplate as a commitment. But I didn't care that much for him: he was quite amusing, and of course rich, but I could not imagine making much in the way of a compromise or sacrifice for him – not that he would expect me to – but I would not risk my health hanging around for him like Mimi. I didn't miss him much when he was not around. I didn't yearn for him. I got bored of him very quickly. The thought was quite ridiculous.

But there was someone out there whose hand I had accidentally touched in the dark when my candle was extinguished. Damn it!

The cool travertine tiles chilled my feet and cold air circled my legs and lifted the edges of the bathrobe. I rubbed my hands together to warm them, and headed in to sleep.

THIRTEEN

I t was a beautiful morning when I headed across towards Goodge Street tube station. It was almost too nice to be disappearing underground, but even on a fine day London's traffic and the rudeness of its people spoil everything about the place, making it noisy and stressful, so it was all about getting through it as quick as you could and trying to block it all out – that seemed to be the survival philosophy of Londoners. Pretend it doesn't exist, pretend that other people don't exist, because the minute you acknowledge the reality of existence in the capital it would tip you over into insanity. Coming from Sheffield, it almost seems rude to just ignore people you sit next to, without at least a nod and a smile, if not the full conversation breaking into details of family life, once the compulsory subject of the weather had been dispatched in order to check that the other person was at least human. But here, if you even make eye contact, people assume you're a nutter, if not a mass murderer or a suicide bomber.

There was standing room only on the Tube anyway so the dilemma didn't arise and I had to stand with my head at an angle as I was pressed against the curved part of the carriage near the sliding doors. At least I'd got my steel toe-capped boots on if anyone trod on my toes. A small middle-aged woman glanced at the logo on my HSE fleece then looked up at me as if to check if I was the petty bureaucrat her *Daily Mail* implied I should be. I smiled at her and she blanked me, turning away to study the blackness of the tunnel.

I changed trains twice and got out at Borough. I wasn't quite sure whereabouts on the High Street the site was so I headed south first then, not finding it, retraced my steps in the other direction. The site was obvious as I approached it – a dirty big gap between buildings boarded off. Access to the site was down a side road and it became apparent that the frontage with the High Street was quite small compared to the size of the site extending to the rear. It was a few years since I'd inspected a construction site and there was a risk I could get caught out by my lack of knowledge of the current regulations and construction practice. I'd have to try and avoid specifics – my plan being to take a good look around the site and speak to as many people as possible.

I put on my hi-vis tabard. The site office was at the top of the steps leading up to an upper level of some cabins. I entered with the attitude of someone who had every right to be there. There were several men sat on chairs waiting to be seen by a man stood behind a counter; possibly he was checking permits-to-work for the day. When I entered it was like walking into a very "local" pub and everyone goes quiet and looks around – like that classic scene in *American Werewolf in London*.

'Is the site manager in, please?'

'He's out somewhere.'

'You mean not here or out on the site?'

'He's here somewhere. Who wants him?'

'An inspector from the Health and Safety Executive.'

'If you'll just wait.'

He finished checking the permit he was dealing with, and spoke into his radio. 'McKenzie to control.'

'McKenzie.'

'Visitor for you. HSE inspector. Can you come up to the site office.'

'I'll head down,' I said.

I waited at the bottom of the steps and put my hard hat on to keep the sun off my head. A man in his early forties, steel-rimmed glasses, with a dark beard flecked with white arrived. He clocked the logo on my helmet.

'I was expecting Miss Morgan.'

'Yes. She would normally deal with you, but I have been tasked with some benchmarking work across a number of sites on management arrangements and compliance with employee consultation legislation.'

It sounded a bit lame to me, but was the best I could think of.

'And you are? We weren't expecting another visit so soon.

'Miller.'

'Have you any ID?'

'Of course.' I got out my warrant and flashed it at him.

'May I?' he said, holding out his hand to take the document. He studied it as if suspicious, took out a notebook and made a note.

'And have you got a business card?'

I had hoped not to have to go into so much detail. I handed him one of my cards.

'You're a long way from home.'

'Yes, I'm on secondment. You know how difficult it is retaining staff in London – this permanent pay freeze has killed recruitment and retention. Miss Morgan will continue to be your main point of contact during the build. But this work is separate – it's a high level project, part of Better Regulation Executive work. I believe Miss Morgan next intends coming in for the steel-erection phase.'

He seemed to be reassured, hearing information that chimed with his understanding of what he'd been told. I took out my own notebook.

'If I could just confirm the details: it's MacFarlane construction, and you are Mr McKenzie – the site manager? And how many on site at the moment?'

'Around sixty-five.'

'And how many of those are directly employed by MacFarlane?'

'Only six: me, the permit authorizer, a foreman on each shift, and a surveyor.'

'And the rest?'

'Various contractors: Goosen are doing the concrete, Morris the utilities, drainage is WMC, security is 6G.'

'Okay, good. Can I have a quick tour around the site to get a feel for what the job is first. And I'd like to speak to the MacFarlane employees, please.'

He headed off without acknowledging that request. I followed him into one of the lower cabins where he handed me a sheet of instructions – the usual cover-your-arse safety information.

'When you've read it, sign here. You'll need eye protection and gloves.'

I patted my pocket. I signed, and was given a pass by a security contractor.

'There are vehicles moving about on site today. Please stick with me. Don't wander off.'

Not once had he shown a flicker of humanity. This was the kind
of inspection that made me really tense, but which brought a special
kind of satisfaction when you managed to nail them for something.
You treat me like something you scrape off your shoes and I'll assert
myself with the backing of one hundred and eighty odd years of
history, and with the self-righteousness that comes from trying to
stop what amounts to at least one death each and every week in
your industry, matey-boy. Today though, I was travelling light, no
prohibition notices, and no intention of really doing the job as it was
intended.

I was led through a turnstile and swiped my pass to get in: much
tighter security than any construction site I'd been on. It was more
like a high hazard COMAH site.

'Is this the only way in?'

'To pedestrians, yes. All vehicles have to enter through the
barrier at the back. I'll show you.'

The site was on several levels: a terracing of concrete structures,
a bit like an extensive Roman ruin, except the outlines were in fresh
concrete — of buildings yet to be built — rather than crumbling bricks
tracing the existence of a civilisation long gone.

'Was there much ground work needed beforehand?'

'Yes, quite a bit.'

'What was that — stabilisation work?'

'Some old cellars and tunnels to fill, crumbling sewers — and it's a
nightmare anywhere in London trying to find accurate records of
what's down there.'

'I can imagine.'

We went round the perimeter of the site past where a crane was
lifting concrete buckets for pouring into shuttered off columns. It
looked a really tidy, well-run site. I told him so and he just sniffed,
as if to indicate, "tell me something I didn't know, you prat." He
wanted this over as quickly as he could manage.

'Is all the piling work completed?'

'Yes, some of it was quite complex.'

At the back of the site was an area for two or three vehicles to
queue before being allowed past the barrier by security. He
introduced me to his foreman — big ugly Cockney by the name of

Mick Hanlon, something like Brutus off Popeye, or one of those rugby league players whose neck is as thick as their head. He didn't say much except play the monkey to McKenzie's organ grinder and complain about how many inspections they were getting off various bureaucrats and council officials.

We were soon back at the cabins again – as his whistle-stop tour concluded.

'Is that it? Only I've things I need to do.'

'I'd like to see your plans for the safety of various phases of the build, and also speak to some of the contractors. What time is their break?'

He checked his watch: 'Half an hour.'

'Okay, if you could dig out those plans and I'll take a look.'

He took me upstairs and through to a cabin that was obviously his office: ex-military it seemed from the photographs on the filing cabinet. He unlocked a cabinet, pulled out some files, locked it again, and placed them on the desk.

'I'll leave you to it.'

I shuffled them around for half an hour, looking for anything vaguely interesting, then headed back out. McKenzie had disappeared. I asked the permit authoriser where the welfare cabin was and he indicated downstairs, back through the turnstile.

I went down and found the cabin: there were a couple of dozen men inside queuing at a large tea urn, then finding a seat or going to stand outside. McKenzie came in.

'You shouldn't have come through unaccompanied.'

'You had disappeared. I wanted to talk to the lads.'

'Feel free, we have nothing to hide. Not many of them will understand you.'

He stood waiting for me to make a fool of myself.

'On their own, please.'

'For what reason?'

'So that they can speak to me uninhibited.'

'By what authority?'

'By the authority I have under the Act to interview people as I see fit. By the authority of this warrant.' I waved the calf-skin wallet at him.

He turned and left. I took off my hat.

'Morning fellas,' I said. 'I'm a government safety inspector. It's nothing to worry about. I'd just like a quick word to check everything's all right on site.'

I got lots of blank looks and several of them ignored me. This wasn't going well. 'Is anyone in here English?'

No one spoke. 'What nationality are people?' I asked one of the few men who was paying me any attention.

'Polish, Hungarian, Latvian, Lithuanian, – and he – and he – they Slovakian.'

The man who spoke looked Eastern European – some look as if they could be English but I always thought there was something in the eyes sometimes, something not quite Anglo-Saxon.

I tried my one word of Polish, learnt on the five-a-side pitches.

'Kulwa! How do you communicate?' he laughed. 'I'm not wanting to cause any hassle, just check that you lads are being looked after okay, that the bosses are treating you fair.'

'Gabor, come here.' A stocky man in his late twenties approached. 'This guy is good guy,' he said pointing at me. I smiled.

He said something to him in whatever language it was.

'I am Radek,' the first man said. 'This is Gabor.'

I shook their hands.

Gabor spoke: 'This good work – tough bosses, but pay okay.'

'I take it there are no unions?'

They laughed. 'You must joke. No unions. No way. You get sack if you mention union. Here, you want tea? Get him tea, Gabor. Sit, sit.'

'I'm also trying to find out about an accident a few weeks ago. It might have been an accident. Do you know anything of it? Don't mention it to the bosses though. I'm trying to keep it, you know, unofficial. It's delicate.'

'I not heard nothing. Have you Gabor? About accident?'

'Can you ask the others for me? See if anyone knows anything?'

They both went off to speak to the others and suddenly the room grew more animated, and people kept looking at me. I smiled and tried to look trustworthy and on their side – not menacing or official. Quite a lot to achieve by use of body language, but I gave it my best shot.

I saw the foreman – the big Brutus – hanging around outside. I shut the door and sat back down and waited. The animation died down and Gabor and Radek returned.

'No one know nothing. Sorry friend.'

'Okay, thanks guys. Appreciate that.'

The door opened, it was the foreman glowering in.

'Looks like tea break over,' Radek said. 'Back to it.'

I shook his hand and Gabor's, then stood up, downing the rest of the disgusting, sweet, milky tea – there are times when you just have to ignore veganism – like that time in France when a Moroccan student presented me with a dish of veal as a special honour – what's that line in *Ratatouille*? "You have to muscle your way past the gag reflex."

I let the rest of the workers file out past me. One or two shook my hand on the way out. A good-looking man – but with dark scraggy hair, several days stubble and a missing front tooth was last out, he shook my hand too. I felt something in my hand – the corner of a newspaper. I slipped it into my pocket and left the cabin as well. McKenzie was waiting outside.

'Got what you needed?'

'Waste of time really – none of them speak English well do they?'

'I told you.'

'Never mind. I can always come back with an army of interpreters.'

He looked at me as if he wasn't sure whether I was joking.

He stared at me. 'I phoned your office and spoke to Miss Morgan. She knows nothing of your visit. Said it was odd.'

'Oh? No – she might not I suppose. We're in different teams you see. Mine is more of an over-arching role. My internal audit team don't always let the local team know – it's a policy thing.'

He was still staring at me.

'Well, I've got all I need for now. I'll leave you to get on. If there is anything else I'll be in touch. Thanks for your time.'

He escorted me to the turnstile and stood outside the office.

'I'll take your pass and sign you out.'

'Thanks. Nice to meet you.' It wasn't at all, you shithead.

I removed my hi-vis and stuffed it into my helmet and only once round the corner did I pull out the piece of newspaper that had been burning a hole in my pocket. It was a corner torn off *The Sun* with a mobile number scribbled on it.

FOURTEEN

I spent the afternoon wandering round the British Museum before returning to my hotel. I took the corner of newspaper and tapped the number into the phone that Abdi had given me – I was just building up to what I'd say when it went through to voicemail. I ended the call: I didn't want to leave a message.

I pulled my trainers back on and headed out to find something to eat – perhaps from a supermarket to bring back to my room and watch some banal nonsense on the telly. As I got out into the street the phone rang in my pocket.

'Hello? It's Peter. I missed call from you.'

'Did we meet at the building site this morning?'

'Yes. You want to talk? You want to know about accident? It not accident.'

'Yes. What can you tell me?'

'No, not phone. You know Coach and Horses in Tottenham. I meet you there in one hour, yes?'

'Er. Yes. Okay. I'll find it. Thanks.'

If I'd had my own phone rather than this ten-year-old Nokia, I could have used that to find out where I was going. I'd have to find it using old-fashioned methods, like asking people – if I could I find a Londoner who would talk to me.

I found White Hart Lane on the Tube map, figuring that must be Tottenham. I'd been there a few years back when we played Spurs in the League Cup and remember it was odd how the ground wasn't actually on White Hart Lane at all.

I thought the train would have been okay at that time of day: easing off since it was gone six, but it was just as bad as it had been in the morning. I had to do that rude London-thing of shoving my way into the carriage to get on. If I'd behaved like a Sheffielder, avoided all physical contact, and been polite, I would have been waiting for a long time, watching others pile on as every train went past full. *Under a Banner* on my iPod helped calm my sense of claustrophobia; as the train slowed and accelerated the only thing stopping me falling over was being pressed against other people. I had to change trains at Seven Sisters onto an equally busy train.

It was good to get back out in the evening air. I followed signs for the football ground, assuming the pub would be in that direction and found a chirpy Cockney who told me it was "up di Oi Rowd."

I walked past Polish and Turkish supermarkets, betting shops, phone shops and various fast food outlets.

The pub was a London boozer – probably awful on match days but early on a Friday evening not too bad. I was a bit early so went to the bar and ordered a pint, then sat near the door so I could see who came in; I couldn't remember what he looked like, this Peter feller.

It was him who clocked me first when he came in. I got up to shake his hand and buy him a drink.

'My name is Mitch, by the way.'

'Peter.'

'Thanks for giving me your number.'

I followed him to a quiet corner of the pub. He sat forward on a stool, hands clasped round his lager, like he was stopping anyone from pinching it, his grey eyes keeping a watch over the whole pub. There were still traces of dust in his dark brown hair, from cement or something.

'Are you really safety inspector?'

'Yes, I am.'

'You not police or government?'

'Well, I work for the government, but as an inspector.' I saw his face change to an expression of unease. 'But I have nothing to do with *the* government. We're independent of them – just health and safety of workers, that's all I do. You can trust me, I promise.'

'So why are you interested in this thing you call accident?'

I had to trust him in return, so I told him me and some friends were worried about someone who had gone missing and was last seen on the MacFarlane site just over two weeks ago.

'Who was this man?'

'He was a journalist. An anti-fascist who was strong on workers' rights. We don't think he just went missing.'

'Are you and your friends on left? Anti-fascist?'

'Yes.'

'Good.'

'So can you tell me anything?'

'The police come round and ask questions too. But I don't trust them. Police are bad in Hungary.'

'Some of ours are good people. But there are bad apples.'

'Apples?'

'It's a saying. Bad apples in a barrel – have to throw them out or they all rot.'

'Yes. I think in Hungary we have something the same: *A rossz barát, rossz útra visz* – it mean a bad friend take you on a bad path. Well I saw real bad apple – someone not to follow on the path. Saw something bad. Was your journalist about forty?'

'Yes. With quite long hair down to his shoulders – a bit scruffy looking perhaps, but not bad looking.'

'Yes, it was probably him. It was a Wednesday. Two week ago. I remember because it was my cousin's birthday.'

'That sounds right.'

'There was shouting. I down trench – had to finish shutters for concrete chamber so I stay longer – rest of men had gone for day. I heard shouting so I climb ladder and look out. There was foreman – you know foreman – big man.'

'Hanlon, was it?'

'Yes him. Nasty. Him shouting at your friend, journalist. I keep head down – not want them to see me and get in trouble. Then I look out slowly – took my white hard-hat off so not be seen, and journalist now pointing at foreman. I still not hear what they say but he laugh at foreman and turn away to go and foreman pick up timber and thud into journalist on head. Then he drag him up and throw him into hole. I was very scared now. If he seen me, he kill me too. I don't know what to do. Not safe to come out. Later I heard wagon arrived and concrete pouring – I worry they come across to where I was too. Lights came on for night shift. I stay in hole for hours. I sneak out when I get my chance, when it break time for night shift guys. I look for hole where threw man but it was new concrete base.'

'You mean he's buried under the concrete?'

'I don't know if he still there. But it possible. Police never find him.'

'Would you tell this to the police?'

'No way. I lose job. I even get killed too. I tell you because you are good guy – comrade.'

'Look, I'm getting hungry. Have you eaten yet? Can I get you something to eat?'

'It is okay, I got food in the house.'

'Go on, let me. I don't want to eat on my own.'

'Very well: we buy something and take it to my flat, yes?'

'Sounds good.'

'There is good kebab place.'

'I don't eat meat.'

'Domino's Pizza?'

'Don't eat cheese, and I'm boycotting them for some reason – forgotten why. The way they treat their workers, I think. Oh! and because back where I live in Sheffield they make these poor people stand on a roundabout all day with signs on their front and back advertising pizza: how is that acceptable to employ human beings to do the same job as wooden posts? I bet they're paid a pittance too.'

'Pittance?'

'It means not much – crap money.'

'You right. No pizza. What about Chinese?'

We talked football while we waited – he supported Ferencevaros – he had to teach me how to pronounce it. I had had some interest in them since Sheffield United had a link with them at one time: the same ownership or something, when we were riding high before it all turned to rat-shit, helped along by West Ham flouting the rules and the football aristocracy closing ranks against us. Peter was less than enthusiastic about his club.

'It has been ruined – the new owner – a right-wing politician sold out on Stadium: it used to be named after a Fradi hero: Florian Albert – you know him? Now it named after sponsor.'

'Happening everywhere, Peter. It's capitalism first, football second, or maybe even third. It no longer belongs to the fans. I shan't even watch the World Cup in Qatar – the whole thing stinks and you know, they say there will be way more people killed building the stadiums than will play in the tournament? I want no part in that. Every one of those fans who turns their TV on to watch will have blood on their hands. Quietly collaborating in FIFA's stink.'

It was only a short distance from the Chinese to Peter's flat: set back from the High Road down a turn-off. The stairs up to his flat weren't particularly pleasant – stale air from several flats and smells of cooking of various nations combined with god-knows-what.

Peter's flat did not surprise me – it was poorly furnished and the carpet was shot. The room we entered contained a small table, a settee and a kitchenette consisting of a gas cooker, a tiny worktop, a sink and an old fridge, all squashed together by the only window. The bedroom was off to one side.

'Hey, this is all right,' I said. 'Got everything you need.'

'It's okay. Expensive though.'

I nodded. I bet he paid as much in rent as I paid for my mortgage in Woodseats.

'Can I use your bathroom?'

'Go ahead. I get plates out.'

'So why did you decide to help me?'

'What happened to your friend was not right, and you and me both socialist, yes? I see people in my village treated bad and killed – just for being Rom. They talk about Rom – gypsy – problem like it is disease. They want to get rid of gypsy in Hungary. I speak out against Magyar Garda – fascists with guns – Nazis. My life in danger there so I come here – Hungary not nice place right now – many fascists in parliament. I have to keep my head down – like in that hole at building site – all the time. I say nothing, they ignore me.'

'It's certainly a worrying time – here too. Racists coming out of the closet after the referendum.'

'No, here is good. Compared to Hungary.'

'Don't be so sure. That journalist was called Mark Tyler – we don't think what happened to him was just a random killing. He was investigating links at the highest level in the UK government with fascists, just as bad as yours but perhaps wearing Church's shoes rather than jackboots.' He looked puzzled. 'Posh shoes – fascists in posh shoes – not boots and Nazi salutes. We know they are going round killing trade unionists – Tyler was also in the NUJ – the journalists' union. They have murdered at least four now – all to stop Labour under Philpott getting into power.'

'I didn't know.'

'Why would you. No one's going to say anything. We do fascism in a very British way – all very polite and without making a silly fuss. We have to fight them on another level. These groups have links as well, you know; they see themselves as fighting for a European race.'

'In Hungary it is more about hatred of Rom and Jews.'

'God! Does history never tell us anything. I need another beer, you got any?'

'No. I don't have beer in house, or I just drink it.'

'Okay. I'll be back in a tick.'

'You get me cigarettes as well? I pay you.'

'What sort?'

'Cheapest. Always the cheapest – my… er…filozofia in life!'

I went back out onto the High Road and found a general store where they sold cold beer from a fridge. I bought us two each and a packet of fags and headed back to Peter's flat.

The door up from the street was still open – I must have forgotten to pull it to. I climbed the stairs to his flat, two at a time. The door to his flat was open too.

'I'm back, Peter. I got you Superkings, I hope that's okay.'

There was no reply. He was sat with his back to me, at the table where I left him. I put the cans on the table.

'Peter? You nodded off?'

I looked at him. He was staring straight ahead. I shook his shoulder and then noticed a damp patch on the front of the black hooded top – I touched it and it left my fingers red. I felt his neck – no pulse. I panicked and flew back down the stairs and out into the street. I started running on the adrenaline, but I saw a police car and stopped, realising how suspicious that made me look. I walked quickly towards the Tube instead.

I phoned Abdi to tell him what had happened, as I turned into White Hart Lane. He was with Josh when I phoned, and he put him straight on to me. I told him about Peter and Mark Tyler.

'Okay, Mitch. Calm it down. Look around you. Are there any cars coming towards you?'

'Loads. There's loads on the road. It's traffic for fuck's sake!'

'Okay, forget that. Do you think anyone's following you?'

'I don't know, maybe.'

'Can you see any taxis? If you can flag one down, do it.'

'Okay.'

'How did you contact this Peter?'

'On my phone, this one.'

'Right you need to ditch this phone quickly, in case they've got his and use it to trace you – take the battery out and lose the phone. Good luck mate. Call us later.'

I looked around me for assassins in mirror-windowed Mercedes, or walking down the street in black paramilitary gear as I fumbled to get the back off the phone then dropped it down a grate. A black cab with its light on was coming towards me on the other side of the road so I'm madly flagged it down like it was a passing ship and I was on a desert island. It did a u-turn and I jumped into it.

'Take me into London please.'

I watched Mitch and his friend in the Chinese takeaway slapping each other on the shoulder and laughing like they were old mates. Now if that was me that would all be an act. If I'd just met somebody and wanted something off them I too could be charming and come across as interested in the other person – but I would just be putting it on, whilst actually despising them. But Mitch is not like that, it is clear he sees the best in people and when he displays a sign of affection or good humour, he is just being Mitch, and means it. What a dreary part of London this was – reminiscent of Rotherham in so many ways.

I followed them up the High Street and watched as they turned down a side street and headed for some flats just set back from the main road – nasty characterless flats built at least expense – using the cheapest of materials and the most basic architectural design. I saw them pass a window on the first floor landing and head up, then a moment or two later lights came on on the second floor.

I phoned in and asked to speak to Choo-choo, who was in charge of the Lincoln's Inn office.

'I've located Miller and he appears to have made a landing – at least for now – just seen returning with a takeaway meal –entering a flat with a man: twenties, Eastern European-looking, so far as I can tell – I didn't want to get too close to them. Likely he's from the MacFarlane site – he looks like a builder.'

'Good work, what's the address?'

'I'll send you the location and a couple of photographs of the flat as well.'

'Good. You should withdraw now and let me deal with it from here.'

'What will you do with him?'

'That's none of your concern. Thank you. A pleasure speaking to you as always.'

I felt a chill run down me as I heard those words. It was clear why it was none of my concern and why I had been ordered to withdraw. What had I done?

I had to be sure of the outcome, if only for my own sanity. They would never tell me, and the thought of not knowing – of having no closure – was too much.

I put my headphones on and played some Justin Timberlake – I know, don't judge a girl by her taste in music, but when he's in a dinner jacket I wouldn't say no.

A scruffy-looking Renault Megane turned into the street and the driver looked across at me. He moved on and turned at the end of the road and came back, slowed down as he passed, wound down his window and looked at me again.

'Piss off, pervert!' I said.

'Bitch!' he shouted and pulled away. If I had had my handgun actually in my hand rather than concealed beneath my blouse I would happily have used it: the fat ugly bastard.

Justin calmed me down by telling me to just "dance, dance, dance." I was a little conspicuous so I moved over the road and stood behind some wheelie bins set back from the street. Just as I did so, I saw the door to the flat open and Mitch came strolling out with a daft smirk on his face like he was – in his head – still enjoying a joke. I ducked down and saw, through the gap between the bins, his jeans and trainers pass by. I watched him turn into the High Street. Should I phone it in? I was just getting my phone out of my jacket pocket when a black VW turned into the road, stopped, then drove past me and parked facing back out, half on the pavement. Two men got out, both wearing scruffy t-shirts, one with a baseball cap the other in naff, white-framed shades. They went into the flat then about three minutes later came back out, looked around and drove quickly off. Mitch rounded the corner soon after swinging a white plastic shopping bag and went back to the flat. Should I say something to him? Would the VW return? Mitch burst back into the street moments later, running. I came out from behind the bins and followed. He was out of sight when I turned onto the main road. It didn't take much imagination for me to realise what he was running from.

My phone rang.

'It's Benny. You gave us some duff gen.'

'No, I didn't.'

'Miller wasn't there.'

'He was when I phoned in. He was settled in for some time with his supper.'

'Well he must have left without finishing it.'

'Don't blame me if your people blew it.'

'Where will he be now?'

'How should I know?'

'You're the one who's been following him all bloody day – you must know.'

'Leave it with me, I'll go back and see if I can pick up the lead.'

'No. Stay well away. Find where he's gone, but that contact is now cold. Where was he staying in London?'

'I'm not sure,' I lied. 'I'll find out.'

'Is there something else?'

'No. Look, I said I'll find out – trust me, there's no way he can outsmart me.'

'You'd better be quick, given events. Before he does something to cause embarrassment.'

Benny's and Choo-choo's intentions were clear – Mitch was now a confirmed live target. I knew the hotel he was staying at, and yet I'd not let on. That's surely where he'd run to and I could still hand him to them on a plate.

I flagged down a cab into town rather than phoning for a driver.

'Gower Street, please.' I told the driver.

'Apologies for the smell, darling. Had a family of our swarthy cousins in the back, if you know what I mean. All bloody immigrants around here. Hardly recognise the place now.'

I just nodded. I do not engage in conversations with servants or cab drivers.

I went straight into the hotel – I had to buzz to be let in.

'Good evening, sorry to bother you. My cousin said he was staying here – a Mr Miller? Can you tell me which room he's in?'

'Miller you say?' He went down the hand written list in his book with his finger.

'He checked in yesterday, he might have just got back in the last half hour or so?'

'No, sorry. No Mr Miller.'

'He's about thirty, sandy hair, about this high, cute, nice smile.'

He looked at me: 'I'm sorry.'

'Can I just look down your list, I'm sure he must be there.'

'I can't let you do that,' he said, closing it.

I went back out and sat on the steps of the neighbouring hotel. I'd tried to read the upside down list of residents as the manager, or whoever he was, was scanning it, but I couldn't make it out. I was obviously not the only one using a pseudonym. He must have come back here – or perhaps he'd still not got back yet – if he'd not come straight back, or if he'd made his way down to the Tube at Seven Sisters or got the Overground? His rucksack must still be in the hotel. When he'd left earlier he had had nothing with him.

It was a pleasant afternoon we'd spent together in the British Museum – getting to know him better – sharing his interest in the things he looked at – okay so I'd stalked him, and only looked at the things he'd looked at after he'd moved on to the next cabinet, but still… I got to wonder why he spent so long looking at some of the objects. Why he spent so long admiring the headless statue of an Egyptian queen wearing a diaphanous robe revealing her breasts, and slightly rounded belly was obvious. The statue, thousands of years old, was enough to turn Julian Clary on. But he also spent a lot of time looking at Greek sculptures of men as well as women. It seems to be people that Mitch was interested in: Lindow man he studied for ages: the upper half of a two thousand year old corpse. A bit gross if you ask me, but also things like funny little figurines made out of clay, or Neolithic representations of women: all hips and bust. Neolithic porn more like. Poor Mitch: obviously not getting enough.

Just as I was wondering what to do next Mitch came out of the hotel, down the steps into the street – I kept my head down. I could see him out of the corner of my eye looking around – he walked straight past me. I got up and followed him across the road towards Waterstones. I didn't know what I was going to do. He turned the corner and went to a phone box. God, he must be desperate – I have never used one of those of vile things. He was on the phone for several minutes. He came out of the phone box and headed back in my direction. I stepped in his way and looked up at him. He stopped and stared.

'But… Jade? You look different. Where…? Are you here for work? What…?'

'Nice to see you again, Mitch.' I reached up and kissed him on the cheek. He looked hurt.

'I didn't like the way you just left like that. I felt used.'

'I know. I'm sorry. I've got a lot of explaining to do. Is there somewhere we can talk?'

'There'll be a pub round here somewhere, or we could get a coffee in Waterstones – no it's shut.'

'Can we…? Can we go somewhere private?'

'I guess… Did you mean…? My hotel's just round the corner.'

'Yes that would be good.'

'Let's get something to drink then, there's a supermarket just along here – it's like… organic stuff – perhaps not your thing Jade?'

'No. Sounds good.'

Mitch picked up some bottles of beer and I added a bottle of Belize rum.

'That's nearly sixty quid,' he said.

'I know. It's my treat, and I might need it. It's on expenses.'

He went into the hotel first to make sure the coast was clear; then sneaked me in after him, up the stairs to his pokey little room on the second floor that was barely bigger than a cupboard.

I didn't hang back, he'd barely put the bottles down before I overwhelmed him – gave him no chance. I just jumped him and closed my mouth around his. I wrapped my legs around him and he fell back with my weight on to the bed.

'Oi, careful. You'll get me thrown out.'

'Shut up, Mitch. No talking.'

Any rational or analytical thought had been put in a barrel, charged with semtex and detonated. I didn't want to think. I was pure instinct. I pushed him back and undressed him and he just lay there smiling up at me and slowly turning pink in the cheeks as I had my way with him and he struggled to contain himself. And then, the poor, sweet boy started to cry: big tears started to roll down his cheeks and he let out a sob. And the sob turned into a laugh, and then he buried his head in my neck and held me so tight that nothing else mattered.

I got into the little bed afterwards and pulled the sheet over me.

'I'm thirsty now,' he said, and got up to fetch the drinks and a bottle opener off his keyring, while I lay back and admired his back and his backside from an angle I'd not seen before, with all the aestheticism of a visitor to the Greek sculptures in the museum.

He pulled back the net curtains. 'It's raining.'

'Mitch, you're naked, someone will see you.'

He shrugged, shut the curtains, passed me a teacup and poured me some beer while he drank from the bottle.

'I'm allowed to speak now then am I?' he said. I smiled at him.

'It's good to see you again Jade, really. But please don't just sneak out on me again. It would break me. Promise?'

'Promise. And it's not Jade. It's Kate.'

'Kate? Why? What do you mean?'

'My real name is Kate. And have you not noticed there's no Mackem accent any more?'

'Oh yeah.' He giggled. Very cute.

'Look, Mitch, I've got a lot of explaining to do, and you are going to end up hating me for it. Just hear me out will you? Then you can leave and never have to see me again, but I want you to know I have really enjoyed being with you despite everything. I have never... made love... to anyone like you. I have had plenty of meaningless shags, but I have never *made love* to anyone until I met you.'

'Are you saying you love me?' He looked me deep in the eyes. A look that penetrated to my core.

'Perhaps... I think so, yes. I think so.'

'You think so? You mean you don't know?'

'Just go easy on me. This is all new to me. I am only here now because I couldn't go on with it. You have really got under my skin, Mitch. I can honestly say I've never felt like this.'

I opened the bottle of rum and put some into the teacup and passed it to Mitch who drained it and passed it back.

'I've been trying not to think about you, Jade – Kate. I can't think of you as Kate. Sorry – Jade has just been going round in my head and I've kept pushing her away because it hurts so much. I don't know why. It makes no sense. We didn't… don't, even know each other. And yet no one so gorgeous has ever taken a second look at me and if I could spend the rest of my life here with you in this room I would. I couldn't hate you no matter what it was you have to tell me. You say you think you love me. I *know* I love you.'

'Don't say that. You'd better hear it first. I wish I were Jade, then things would be so much easier.'

'Then stay, Jade. You don't have to be Kate.'

'That's sweet. If only life were that simple. But the fact is you're in a hell of a lot of trouble. Someone is trying to kill you.'

'How do you know that? What…?'

'I'll get to that, but I can't let that happen. I want to help you. I know what happened to Mark Tyler. I know what happened to your friend today.'

'It was horrible. I have seen dead bodies at industrial sites, where the scene is being preserved or it is unsafe to retrieve the body. But today – someone I'd just been talking to… And he was a good man. But how…? How do you know?'

'It's a long story.' I poured some more rum. 'What do you know about the Perceval Group?' He listened in silence until I got to the bit where I said I was sent to Rotherham.

'Wait… No! You can't be…' He scrabbled out of bed.

'No, Mitch, please.'

'You fucking bitch. It was you! Sharon!'

I tried to hold him back but he pushed me away, and then something happened to me that hasn't happened since I was a little girl and my horse became lame and had to be shot – I cried. Not just a theatrical tear summoned up from imagined self-pity, but something raw and uncontrolled. It took me by surprise and I sobbed and my whole body convulsed as I let go. I cried for Mitch and for me, for Mimi and Rodolfo.

'I'm so, so, sos…sos…sorry. I'm so sorr…r..y.'

He sat next to me on the bed and I buried myself in him and sobbed and sobbed.

When my tears had run dry I uncurled myself from him. My head was against his chest and I saw he was aroused again. I reach out gingerly to touch him and he let out a shiver.

'How fucking could you?' he said, as he pushed me back onto the bed. 'How fucking could you?' He lay on top of me and I let him enter me and he shagged me in as rough a manner as I have ever been shagged before. Almost as if in revenge or hate, but it was okay, I wasn't scared, I welcomed it. It was a catharsis – for both of us.

He lay still on top of me afterwards and I gently stroked his hair.

'They're going to kill you too,' he said into the pillow. I wriggled under the dead weight. He rolled off me. I looked him in the eye.

'What do you know about Plan D or the Fourth Way?' he said. 'Do you know who killed Vernon-Harcourt?' It was now my turn to listen. I poured more rum.

'So what are we going to do?' I said.

'I've not got a fucking clue,' he said. 'I need to speak to someone… Abdi… get advice. No, I can't do that. This is War. Normal rules don't apply. I'm too fucking drunk to think.'

'Me too, Mitch. Can't think at all. Let's leave thinking to the morning.' I snuggled into him and wove my legs around his.

SIXTEEN

Early on Saturday morning a waitress came out of the basement door of a London hotel for a smoke. She climbed the steps and passed her cigarette packet to a man leaning against the railings. He in turn took out a cigarette along with two keys and slipped a tight roll of £20 notes into the packet. The waitress went back down the steps.

A Transit van pulled up outside, the driver put on his *park-anywhere* hazard lights and two men in jeans and T shirts got out. The man who had been leaning against the railings, smoking, approached them, shook hands with one, then departed. The two men from the van climbed the steps to the hotel, opened the front door with a key and made their way up to the second floor.

They paused briefly outside room 11, then slid a key into the lock and entered.

In the dim light inside one of the men accidentally kicked a glass bottle sending it clattering into another bottle.

'What the fuck! Jade!'

The two men pounced and rolled the naked man out of the bed onto the floor before he was fully awake. One put a foot on the man's bare back and placed a handgun to his head before he could catch his breath. The other man trained his gun on the woman in the bed so that it was the first thing she saw when she opened her eyes.

The naked man tried to struggle but was kicked until he stopped. Whilst keeping his gun trained on the woman the man sorted through the pile of clothes at the end of the bed and removed a holster, phone, money, everything from pockets, and threw the clothes onto the bed.

'Time for Romeo and Juliet to leave their love nest. Get dressed.'

The men observed closely as the woman got dressed; then she was handcuffed behind her back. The man on the floor was kicked again for fun then ordered to get dressed too.

'Jade?' The woman didn't speak; she shook her head slightly and pleaded with her eyes.

'Shut up if you want to survive. Both of you.'

Within minutes of its arrival, a white Transit van was heading out of London up Finchley Road, just one of many such vans skirting round and dipping into the congestion zone that day, largely ignored, occasionally cursed by cyclists and other drivers. Mostly they carried out honest trade, but how many concealed something less innocent behind their grimy panels? How many carried the products of theft, or goods untaxed by the Revenue, or simply derived from exploited labour somewhere in the world? How many concealed illegal immigrants or modern slaves?

The white Transit van heading towards Brent Cross had two in the front and three in the rear: two lying on the floor of the van with tape over their mouths and hoods over their heads, and a man sat on a bean-bag, smoking and keeping watch, a loaded gun in his hand.

SEVENTEEN

I adjusted my position as best I could to ease the pain. I had been lying on this cold floor in my own piss for hours. I had reconciled myself to my death – the pain was immense: in my sides from where I had been kicked, in my neck and head from lying here and on the metal floor of the van, and from the almighty hangover I was suffering from. It was thudding like I'd never known, and I felt sick, but I knew I mustn't be. With the tape over my mouth, it could be the way I died – choking on my own vomit: not a nice way to go, but I suppose at least it would be over with.

I was alone as far as I could tell. It had been quiet since I was pushed out of the back of the van onto the floor here; I heard it pull away, no words were spoken, and a manual, roller-shutter door was closed. The last thing being its chain clanking as it swayed to a stop. Then silence.

It was a large room with hard surfaces from what I could tell from the sounds I made from what little tapping I could make with my feet. There was no reply to the "Mmm" noises I could make with the gaffer tape over my mouth.

I didn't know where Jade – or Kate – was. We had stopped five minutes before I was taken here and she was dragged out of the van. I heard her moan as they bumped her into something; then the doors were shut again.

From such a high to such a low. Logic tells me I had been betrayed by her, that I had been incredibly stupid to let my dick rule my brain. All that stuff she told me about her involvement with the Perceval Group had just been a ruse: the sacrificing of a pawn or two in her strategy to get everything from me and then to hand me over to her dodgy mates. And yet – why had they treated her so badly as well? Probably to make it look convincing, to keep me guessing, to make me think there was still some hope for me somewhere.

Come on Mitch, think! I couldn't get logical thoughts out. Why had they not just killed me already and dumped my body? They must still have some use for me – or want something more off me.

Do they think I know more than I do? Know something more of the Fourth Way? What did I have that would be useful to them? What did I know: Abdi? Josh? I knew a bit about Abdi, but nothing about Josh really – I didn't even know if those were their real names. I knew little else. How long before they knew I was in trouble? When I called Abdi from the phone box, I told him what had happened: about how Mark Tyler died, about Peter, and said I'd head back to Sheffield in the morning. By lunchtime they'd start wondering where I was. But there was nothing they could do. They knew which hotel I was at, but that was it. No one had seen me leave so far as I was aware – except, possibly, the few people in the street at that time – perhaps, to them, two people being put in the back of a Transit van would look odd? They might report it, if they had not been ignoring all humanity in their little iPhone bubbles.

Would Kate really have confessed to me about the things she'd done if she hadn't been genuine? What would her motive have been? All she got out of me of any substance was that I knew she was a target, and that Vernon-Harcourt had been target number one before her – but everyone probably knew that anyway except for the press and public, who as ever were kept in the dark – mushrooms, that's what they were, kept in the dark and fed on manure.

She hadn't spoken to me, just gave me a look as I dressed – a look those thugs didn't see – a look that said: "Be still my love. Believe me." Or am I just going mad?

Oh, how I wish I had some sort of faith – someone to pray to, or someone I believed had a purpose in all this. I don't want to lie here for days like this, slowly dying.

I expect the pain will increase – is that how it happens or does the body just start to shut itself down bit by bit until you drift off to sleep never to wake? Or do you just cry out in pain at the end, begging for it to end? I thought back to my Dad's last few weeks – how he suffered. But was that just because he was a stubborn bastard who would never admit to pain, who would never want to trouble the doctors? A baby-boomer warrior who never had a war to fight – except in his head. A warrior fighting that thing inside him eating him up, and determined to do it alone and with the stiff upper lip of previous generations like his father and grandfather who had fought in proper wars?

It was only when my mother could take no more that he submitted to the humiliation of the medical system – he was defeated and pumped with morphine – he was taken from us from that point on, rarely lucid and even then only wanting one thing: for it all to be over with. Asking why, if there was a God, he would make him suffer like this. I think he was in fear of where he was going to end up. Perhaps religion isn't a comfort at all – it is better to know that death is nothing: that being dead is just like not being born in the first place. We are all insignificant collections of amino acids thrown together by an amazing coincidence of evolutionary events. There is nothing "special" about me – nothing eternal, no spirit except for this collection of cells functioning and neurons firing. In a few days I'll just be dead matter – star dust recycled somewhere – carbon atoms returning to the soil or floating up into the atmosphere to contribute to the destruction of this bloody awful mess of a planet. One fewer great ape for Mother Nature to have to deal with.

I still battle with my guilt over wanting him to die faster. Not just because that's what he wanted, though that was all I'd admit to. If I were to be honest, his illness had become a great inconvenience, and a worry as I watched my mother struggle to cope. I'd spent weeks in a state of guilt over our relationship as he was dying – but it was too late to say anything. Somehow something went wrong between us when I reached secondary age. Was it me, or was it him? When I was his little boy, and looked up to him and hero-worshipped him, he was content. But then, when I started to be my own person, my own man, he recoiled and withdrew. As if by rejecting his faith and his wishy-washy, liberal politics, his views on life, by revealing his lack of knowledge when it came to my homework, he felt rejected too, and wasn't emotionally intelligent enough to deal with it. I probably didn't help the situation, but I was the child still. He should have been able to deal with it as a grown up. We stopped doing stuff together – I went to matches with my mates, shunned his company because we'd always end up arguing. And his working away meant it was easy to ignore him.

Then, somehow, when I'd grown up it was all too late. He never showed any interest in my achievements or what I'd been up to, and my response was "So what, sod him." If I had lived to be a father I would have done things so differently.

I guess, looking back, he felt threatened and overshadowed, questioned his own achievements. Like so many men: they judge their worth by physical stuff, and titles to their name, not by their networks of friends and family. I suppose I am not immune from that. No matter which way you look at it, not many people will miss me: my cousin Pete, and a few mates from school, one or two from uni I kept in touch with on Facebook and shared a pint or two with sometimes before away games. But no one who would "never get over it": no partner, no kids. My sister would shed a few insincere tears, my mother would make the most of it and revel in the sympathy she would get, but it would be mostly about them. And not much tangible left behind. Perhaps one or two workplaces a bit safer thanks to me, but not much else apart from a Twitter account, and some nice photos on Flickr — accounts that will lie dormant until someone realises and presses "delete."

EIGHTEEN

I was allowed to go to the bathroom. As I sat there I wept for the second time, quietly now. What a bloody mess!

I splashed cold water over my face from the tap and tried to remove the smudges of yesterday's make-up, straighten my hair, make myself look a little more in control. My mouth was sore where the tape had been ripped off. That was the best I could do.

One of the staff from the house was waiting for me outside and led me to a room, exquisitely decorated with dark green William Morris wallpaper at the top half of the walls and oak panelling up to a dado rail below. A man I didn't recognise, suited, reminding me somewhat of a very un-funny Harry Hill, was sat behind a green leather-topped desk. Two chairs were arranged in front. Raife rose from one of them as I entered; Harry Hill remain seated.

'Kate, come in. How's it going?'

'Could be better, Raife.'

'Have they given you a drink, or breakfast? No? That's out of order. Let me ring for something for you.'

'Out of order? They had me bound and gagged and thrown in a van, never mind tea and toast.'

'Sorry to hear that. We'll provide them with some feedback.'

'Feel free to pass me a customer-satisfaction survey form.'

'Kate, this is a colleague. You don't need to know his name. Let's just call him John shall we?'

'Or Harry?'

'If you would rather.'

'Let's cut the crap, Raife. What the fuck is going on? Your goons compromised my operation.'

'What's going on? That's what you need to tell us, Kate. Let's look at the facts. You give a false location on a target. Then you say you don't know where the target is. Then we don't know where you are until you briefly switch on your phone in the night. And you are found in bed with him. It looks to us like you compromised yourself, Kate. That you've got too close to this Miller character.'

'Don't be bloody ridiculous – have you not got a clue how people work, either of you? Are you so bloody Aspergers that you can't see the value of looking someone in the eye and sucking their soul from them to get them to reveal everything?

'I am clearly just too smart for you bunch of amateurs. Miller was exactly where I said he was when I phoned in. If you hadn't sent a pair of clowns we would have got him. If they had been more subtle and watched for a minute or two, or, if Choo-choo had not ordered me to withdraw too early, I could have made contact with the operatives for confirmation. Your guys fucked up, not me. So, you'd made me lose the trail I had worked hard on all day. I had little to go on – I didn't know if he was going to do a runner or not. The only thing I had was that he had left his bag at St Pancras left luggage, so I waited there and followed him back to a hotel. Am I just too subtle for you, is that it?'

There was a knock at the door and a tray with a china teapot, cups and a plate of biscuits and flapjacks arrived. I stuffed one in my mouth so as not to have to speak until I'd collected my thoughts a bit.

'I thought I might as well use my hold over him to find out which room he was in and to get as much information off him as I could: to fully exploit that vein before the mine was closed, so to speak.'

'But, cavorting with the enemy, Kate?'

'Cavorting? Is that what you call it? Is that what they call it at Eton? So, what? are you jealous? Is that it? Both of you? Don't raise your eyebrows at me, Harry. I bet you'd both like a bit wouldn't you?'

I thrust my tits at them and undid a top button.

'Calm down, Kate.'

'Calm down! I've just been trussed up like a bloody turkey at Christmas, battered about by your goons and generally treated like shit, and you tell me to calm down? I'll be as bloody angry as I like, thank you very much.

'What is so wrong with mixing business with a bit of recreation, eh? You types always say your rounds of golf are more to do with business than pleasure. You are surely not so prudish as to make a distinction are you?

'I had confirmation that they were behind George's death.'

'We know that, Kate. That hardly justifies it.'

'No? Well did you know I am next on the list? See, you didn't know that did you? If I hadn't been looking after me who else would have found that out? And you've the audacity to doubt me? There was more he was going to tell me as well, if only you'd not blundered in. Just how much more he knew, we might never know now, but I reckon he knew all about how Plan D was organised – he was much more a player then we had ever guessed – not on the fringes after all. Why don't you let me have another go at him? I could still get somewhere?'

'No, Kate.'

'Where are you holding him? At that old meat factory is it?'

'No, it's not – not there. You don't need to know.'

Raife went so far down in my estimation then, the pupil had become better than the master. I knew he was lying to me. Call it female intuition if you like, but he was practically denying it and yet nodding his head at the same time.

'Don't worry we'll still get it from him.'

'Oh yeah? With as much guile as a pack of hounds in full chase I shouldn't wonder. To get the lid off a new jam jar, often it only takes a tweak from the tip of a teaspoon in the right place rather than the grunting and straining that you boys no doubt employ.'

'All right, Kate. That's enough. We're sorry. We're sorry for doubting you.'

'Right, good. I accept your apology. Now can I have my things back and get on with my job? I need to go and get a new set of clothes, dye my hair and assume a new identity to avoid getting shot, if that's all right with you? I'll report into Lincoln's Inn to get a new passport and a new mission once I've changed my look. Perhaps you could sort me out something in Brussels or New York until things have blown over?'

'We'll see what we can do, Kate.'

I had to move fast. I got a lift to the nearest town with a railway station and went into a pub. I fluttered my eyelashes at the landlord to get him to let me use his mobile – I put a twenty-pound note down on the bar as backup, which he refused.

'I'll need to make quite a long call, so please take it for your trouble.'

He slipped it into the pocket of his pink Lacoste shirt.

Mitch had let slip his mate's name in the pub in Sheffield: Abdi. I'd taken a picture of them together and knew this Abdi had left-wing connections and ran a minicab. Hadn't he mentioned that name again last night? It was worth a try. I googled names of taxi firms in Sheffield and started phoning them:

'Have you got a driver call Abdi? I've a really important message for him.'

'Sorry, love. We've got a few Pakis, as you might imagine: we've a couple of Rajs, a Shiv, an Amerjit, but no one called Abdi.'

On the third attempt – City Cabs – the woman was a bit impertinent: 'Look love, I've got customers trying to get places, I can't be running errands for all the drivers as well.'

'But it is really important. Please. I don't want to overstate it, but a life could depend on it. He'll be really appreciative – likely you'll be rewarded. What's you name?'

'Shirley.'

'Well, Shirley, I'll make sure you are seen right and I'm not just talking a bunch of flowers from the local garage.'

'In that case: we've got an Abdul, and an Abdulaziz – but they're usually "Abdu"s, there is an Abdi-something-or-other who we just call Abdi – it gets a bit confusing. Which one is it?'

I remembered the cab we followed – that would make sense: 'It might be a silver Skoda.'

'That'll be the last one then. Is he a big fella? I'll try and get hold of him for you. Who shall I say wants to get hold of him?'

'A friend of Miller – and he needs help. You got that? Do you need this number?'

'No, we're a taxi firm – it's on the console.'

I ordered a lemonade and some snacks while I waited for what seemed ages.

The iPhone started playing *Eye of the Tiger* – that figured.

'Hello? Is that Abdi?'

'Abdi? Fuck off! No it's Mark, where's Gav?'

'I'm borrowing his phone – can you call back? I'm waiting for a call.'

'No, can you…?' I cut him off.

It rang again. 'Who is this?' the voice said.

'Is that Abdi?'

'Yes, who are you?'

'I'm a friend of Mitch's. He's been abducted by Perceval Group people.'

There was silence at the other end.

'I don't know what you're talking about.'

'For fuck's sake! I'm not playing games here. Do you know about the Fourth Way? If so, can you raise somebody? I know they did for George Vernon-Harcourt. I know what they're capable of. So you must have got what it takes to respond? He is in big trouble. I'm at The Bull in Wheathampstead, just south of Luton. How quickly can you get someone here?'

'How do I know it's not a trap?'

'It isn't, you've got to believe me.'

'Who are you?'

'You're best not knowing. But I am a friend of Mitch's. I might know where he's being held, but we don't have much time to get to know each other, Abdi, please. I care about Mitch. You've got to believe me.'

'Okay. Leave it with me.'

'Be quick, please.'

'Can we use this number?'

'Yes. Ask for Sam – thank you, Abdi.'

I took the phone back to the bar. 'I'm waiting for a call back, maybe. My name is Sam by the way. Oh, and someone rang for you.'

I ordered some food and went out to get some wet-wipes and make-up and a copy of *The Spectator* to read to try to take my mind off things.

I felt a bit more human after I'd eaten. Okay, so a wet-wipe wash in the toilets of The Bull is not the best and washing your hair over a basin with hand soap and drying it with a Worldcorp dryer is not ideal, but needs must.

The wait was awful. I hoped I had given them enough of a suggestion of his usefulness to want to keep him alive – at least for a bit longer.

NINETEEN

Two men came in the bar and looked around – they looked like a pair of hunt-sabs: grungy types. One with a ponytail and combat jacket, the other with more hair on his chin than on his head with a Combat Rock t-shirt and a pair of black trousers which looked like they were bought at Wickes as an impulse purchase at the till whilst buying nailing guns, or whatever it is that they sell.

I got to my feet.

'You Sam?' The big, beardy one said.

I nodded.

'Come with us. I'm Taz and this is Mikey. No messing, yeah?'

'No. This is too serious.'

I got into the passenger seat of the dark blue Peugeot. Taz was driving. 'Where we heading?

'Head south on the B651 to St Albans. I think they might be holding him at an industrial unit not far from here.'

'How do you know this?'

'Inside information, let's say.'

'Nice one. So is your cover blown then.'

'No.'

'Cool.'

'It's complicated.'

'We've not been told much except this guy has got to be sprung, yeah?'

'Yeah. It's important – to the whole project – the whole cause.'

'Glad to be of help them, ain't we, Mikey?'

'Yeah, it's our speciality, helping people.'

'You boys equipped?'

'I think we've got what we need. What we up against?'

'Automatic weapons, standard security systems at the unit, well trained ex-military times.'

'No worries. We've got a little box of tricks in the boot as well.'

'If I'm going to survive this you're going to have to help me out.'

'Okay, Sam. What do you need?'

'You'll need to make it look like you've taken me hostage too. My plan was to lead you up to this place as a trap.'

'Hold on. I don't like the sound of that.'

'Just shut up for a minute – all I want is to get Mitch out alive. So I take you there, not knowing he is there, if you see what I mean. You rescue him – leave me there instead. What can possibly go wrong?'

'How many are we up against?'

'That I don't know.'

'We'll have to find out then.'

'Turn down this lane ahead – after the bend. It's here somewhere, I think. Pull over will you? Just while I get my bearings. Can I borrow your phone?'

I pulled up a map of where we were. 'Yes, we're close. I'll just get out.'

I climbed onto the bonnet of the car to look over the hedge.

'Yes, over there – that's the back of the premises over that field. The front entrance is next left. There will be CCTV at the front gate, as far as I recall, and covering the yard but not at the back – it is just standard from when it was a factory.'

'We'll park up before we reach the gate then.'

'Can I use the new toy, Taz?' said Mikey.

'I think that would be useful.'

We parked in front of an old farm gate and Mikey went to the boot and lifted out a drone, which he placed on the car roof. He switched on the remote control device, which had a built on screen – a bit like a laptop.

'Mikey is an ace with this, he does drone racing competitions. Watch this.'

The drone took off and went over some trees. We watched it disappear and followed it on the screen, looking over Mikey's shoulder – the factory came into view and the drone slowed and hovered over the roof, edging forward as Mikey fiddled with the controls.

'Two cars in the car park.'

'Looks like a van and a Jag. That mean anything to you Sam?'

'No, could be a van for the security man, and visitors in the Jag? Two, maybe three tops, from the house nearby.'

'That's okay. Do you fancy the front or the back Mikey?'

'Can I take out the Jag with the drone?'

'No, let's be subtle, anyway that thing cost a fortune. Blowing it up just to set fire to an empty Jag is not worth it.'

'Shame.'

' 'nother time, mate. No, if you take out the CCTV cameras when I am in position then go in the front way – in fact why don't you blow up the cars as well for a diversion – but just old-school, yeah, with Molotovs, maybe it will bring someone out the front.'

'What shall I do?' I said.

'Why don't you guard the car?'

'What, like a girl?'

'That's what I had in mind.' He smiled at me. 'Only kidding – I'm not like that. But we've not carried out a competence assessment have we?'

'Tell you what: once the cameras are out, so I'm not recognised, why don't I bring the car up to the front gate for you, so you can get away quicker.'

'That's not a bad idea.'

'For a girl, you mean?'

'Yeah, something like that,' he said, laughing at me.

Mikey brought the drone in, landing it gently back down on the car roof. He then packed it away and took out what looked like a fishing rod case and a small rucksack. Taz also got a rucksack out.

'Here's the keys. There's a radio and receiver in the car – I'll just check it – channel three, Mikey.'

'Roger that,' he said into the radio I spotted, built into the strap of his rucksack.

'Not yet, soft lad. Now try.'

The radio crackled: 'Roger that.'

'There you'll be able to keep up with us on that radio.'

My two new best mates set off on their mission: one down the lane, the other over the gate and into the field. It was a nerve-wracking wait.

TWENTY

I don't suppose you've ever tried, but it is almost impossible to
sleep on a solid floor with your hands fastened behind you with
cable ties and with gaffer tape around your ankles strapping them to
something solid so that you can't turn over. I tried my best to relax,
to push thoughts out of my head, to pretend I was somewhere else.
At least I could breathe a bit through my mouth now that I had
loosened the tape with my tongue and by flexing my jaw.

I said I tried to push thoughts away, but I couldn't stop them
breaking through the barrier I tried to construct around my mind. It
had all started with that dead dog in the window. Before that I had
thought I had been politically aware: interested in politics, if not
very politically active in recent years. I'd always voted and always
responded to requests from my union, or to ballots or consultations.
I now realised just how shallow that awareness was – how deep
were those murky waters beneath and what malignancy lurked down
there, swirling around in the gloom, unnoticed and unknown,
surfacing only now and then to devour innocents before slithering
back into waters where light did not penetrate. Up on the surface
were creatures who, duck-like, went about their everyday business,
concerned only where the next piece of bread was coming from,
courting, reproducing, back-biting and squabbling. Were they
innocent, or ignorant, or did they just choose not to enquire beyond
what they saw: because life was just simpler if you pretended the
surface was all there was? And of course ignorance was just what
those dark forces strove to maintain. Had they stopped their prattle
for just long enough to think, they might have wondered how the
currents and climate that affected their lives were created in the
depths, how their universe was but a tiny part of a greater whole.
That those monstrous beings below would rise to feed and cull in
order to exert their power was something that would upset them if
they questioned it, so they did not. They looked for other
explanations for the difficulties they faced, they blamed each other
and their squabbling grew and became more violent as their hatred
and intolerance built.

The sound of an engine brought me to my senses. It stopped and I heard the chain of a roller shutter start to haul the door. Footsteps approached me slowly. Twenty, thirty yards away? They came nearer and stopped. I felt the toe of a boot in my ribs.

'Ha. So you're still alive then? I suppose you'll be wanting a drink?'

I nodded and tried to make an affirmative sound.

'Shame I've not got anything then isn't it?' There was a laugh. 'Shall we get you on your feet?'

I heard the tape around my ankles being cut and felt them come free.

'Up you get then.'

I managed to get up into a sitting position despite the pain in my ribs, but then I could get no further. Had I not felt in such pain – perhaps the normal me – I would have easily been able to jump up. I writhed around.

'Fucking spaz.' He then kicked me over onto my knees with my forehead scraping the cold tiles. I tried to get up onto one knee from there, then pushed up to try to stand. My legs gave way and I fell back onto my knees.

'Let's give you a bit of assistance in standing shall we?' I felt something being fastened to my arms; then I heard another chain being moved, followed by a hoist being operated. There was a sudden jerk as my arms were pulled up my back and an excruciating pain in my shoulders as my weight bore down on them. I struggled up off my knees again to stop my arms being wrenched out of their sockets as I was hoisted up with my wrists – the cable ties biting into my flesh.

'There, that's more like it. Just wait there a bit.' I heard him walking away.

As the blood flow returned to my legs I was able to take my weight on them – and it was an act of necessity to stand as tall as I could to take the weight off my arms, even though I was bent forwards. I couldn't keep it up for long though. I could hardly breathe. I felt dizzy and in such pain: in my shoulders, my neck – everywhere.

'Oh dear, oh dear.'

It was another voice – I'd not heard anyone else approach.

'What a state we're in, Mr Miller.' The bag was pulled from my head. I tried to look up but could only see the floor of the room, the pinstriped trousers and Oxford brogues of a man in front of me. I could see in my peripheral vision that he was wearing a suit.

'Shall we get you a seat? Make you more comfortable?'

I grunted.

'Fetch a chair for our guest.'

There was someone else nearby who moved away; then returned. The hoist was lowered and I collapsed down onto a white plastic chair.

'I am terribly sorry for the way you have been treated.' I could now see the man who spoke – not much older than me, in a navy blue suit – looked a lot like one of those odious barristers who pops up from London to the provinces to defend the indefensible – picks up several thousand pounds for spouting bollocks in clipped tones from under a stupid wig, then buggers off back to London, singing the praises of the British justice system. I've come across a number of these unctuous individuals trying to make out that it was their clients Messrs Bleed'em Dry & Co. Ltd who were the victims of overzealous regulators, despite them having cooked someone alive in an oven or dropped a two tonne piece of metal on top of them. These victims of interference in the free markets, who docked every penny of the deceased's wages they could, including the half day he failed to complete, and who never even sent so much as a bunch of daffs or a cheap Clinton card to the widow.

'Let me remove that tape from your mouth. Must be frightfully bothersome.' He got hold of the corner and ripped it away, with a smile on his face.

'Can we make Mr Miller more comfortable by cutting his bonds?' He spoke to the man behind me who pushed my shoulders forward and cut the cable ties. It hurt to move my arms but it was a relief to adjust my shoulders at last.

'Perhaps we should just make sure he's nice and secure though?'

I was in no fit state to resist as the other man taped my wrists to the chair arms and my ankles to the chair legs. This other man was not of the same type as the barrister – he was older, bald, and looked more like someone who might come round to read your meter.

'There, that's better. I suppose you would like a drink?'

I nodded. 'Please.' My mouth was so dry I could barely whisper. I look around now – it was a former factory unit that had been fitted out for food handling – a tiled floor – walls clad in washable panelling, and a stainless steel table behind me that presumably was the thing my legs had been fastened to.

The gas meter reader went over to a row of steel sinks. I heard a tap running. The thought of water wetting my mouth and passing down my throat was the only thing I could think of. He returned with the filthiest looking plastic jug you've ever seen: God only knows what it had been used for. He passed it to the barrister.

'Here you are.' He held the spout to my lips for half a second – just long enough for me to suck in a teaspoonful. I looked up at his smug face.

'You can have more when you decide to co-operate. Tell us what you know and I'll do what I can to look after you.'

'I don't know anything.'

'Come, come. You can do better than that. I'll be more specific shall I? What do you know about Plan D? Who do you know? I want some names and addresses. Where they meet? – that sort of thing.'

'I told you. I don't know anything. I'm just a safety inspector. They wanted information off me.'

'Who's *they*?'

'They didn't say.'

'Right. This is how it is.' He came right up to me: put his face close to mine. I could smell the garlic on his breath.

'I am the closest thing you have to a friend here in this world. You need me. If you don't tell me what I need to know then I will have to go back to my superiors and tell them. I would have to leave you with this gentleman here – well I say gentleman – being gentle is not one of the things he's renowned for, except when he's handling the baby partridges he breeds. He's a technician, shall we say – he has brought his tools with him in that box – pliers, drills, saws, hammers: those kinds of things. So there are two ways you can do this. It's up to you.' He stood back up.

'Okay. I need a drink.' I whispered. 'My voice…'

He gave me another tiny sip.

'I really am just an inspector. I just passed on some information that's all.'

'We know you're more than just that. My patience has been tried, Mr Miller. Lance help us out. I'll be back soon. Try not to kill him just yet.'

TWENTY-ONE

T he radio crackled. 'I'm in place by the rear fire exit. Over.'

'Roger that. Stand by.'

I waited.

'Shit. Someone's coming out… It's the Jag…'

There was what seemed like a long wait.

'I don't think they saw me. I'm soaking bloody wet in a ditch now. Over.'

I scrambled quickly across to the passenger door and got out. I'd just crouched down at the side of the car when I glimpsed the black Jag approaching. I took the car key out of my pocket, but it didn't have remote locking – the fucking heap of junk – it would have to be locked from the driver's door.

The Jag slowed and stopped as it pulled alongside, and I heard the smooth clunk of a superior car door opening – just one door, thank God. I didn't dare look up. There was a crunch of feet on gravel; then I heard the driver's door of the Peugeot being checked and opened. I felt the car rocking and heard things being thrown around inside as it was searched – had they noticed the radio? The car shook again as the person got out. I dared a peek up through the windows – the man was going round to the boot. If he looked inside he'd see the drone and controls and whatever other equipment or weapons were in there.

I crawled round towards the back and reached under my hooded top. I pulled the pistol and fired just as the man sprung the boot open. He didn't see it coming. I fired again with more accuracy, twice into the chest. He fell backwards, dead.

It was then that I noticed the sharp suit and chiselled features of Raife.

I emptied the boot and managed to heave his body into it – folding him into a foetal position. Poor Raife, but it was him or me.

I radioed in: 'Slight problem, boys. But dealt with – upgraded the getaway vehicle to a Jag. Over.'

'Roger that,' said Taz.

'Camera covering the gate is sorted. I'm going to crop the bolt on the gate and go in now. Standby,' said Mikey.

I locked the Peugeot, started the Jag's engine and reversed it back down the narrow lane towards the gate – it was only two or three hundred yards.

The gate was open as I pulled up to it. I wound the window down to get a better look. Mikey was kneeling down setting up a rifle on a rest to aim it at a camera located over the entrance to cover the yard of the factory. He was concentrating on his task and didn't see a door opening at the building's reception. A man came out, raised a handgun and started running forwards to get in range. I shouted: 'Mikey!'

It was like watching something in slow motion: I saw him pick up the rifle and turn it on the man – then the man fell, and I heard the retort – not loud – a nice weapon.

Mikey placed the rifle back on the rest and fired it again, twice in the direction of the camera. I couldn't see what he had hit but he got up, took something out of his rucksack and walked over to the van – he had bottles in his hand, which he then threw and flames lapped under the van as Mikey ran towards the building. I thought nothing was going to happen – that the fuel was just burning out. Then suddenly there was a further surge of flame – followed by a bang and a whoosh as a fireball engulfed the van.

I opened the gates and drove into the yard – if I were spotted they would only see the car not the driver. A pedestrian door next to a large roller shutter door opened and a bald head looked out and then quickly shut the door again. Mikey dashed towards it, but the door shut before he reached it. I got out and ran to help. Mikey tried the door but it was only openable from the inside.

'There's the main entrance over there,' I said.

We ran over. As we did so there was an explosion.

'That's Taz making his entrance I reckon.'

We went through an empty reception, across a floor littered with dust and unopened letters and looked for the route through to the unit – we went down a short corridor past washrooms and an old clocking-in board, turned right and through a door at the end into the factory unit.

The first thing I saw was Mitch and a lot of blood all down his white T-shirt. Then over to my left was Taz with a gun drawn facing the automatic weapon of the bald man.

'Game over,' said Mikey, aiming at the man. I drew my gun out too, just in case. The bald man started to lower his gun and Taz fired twice straight into his chest.

I ran over to Mitch. There was blood everywhere – splattered all down his front, down the backs of his hands and on the floor. His head had lolled forwards on to his chest.

'Mitch?' I felt his neck for a pulse. He raised his head, saw me and struggled to smile – revealing gaps in his teeth.

'Do you think a good dentist will be able to fix these back in?' he whispered, indicating several bloodied stumps of teeth on the floor.

Taz and Mikey came over.

'Is he okay?' said Taz.

I nodded and smoothed Mitch's hair back from his forehead.

'We've left a bit of a mess here, Mikey,' said Taz.

'And I'm afraid there's another one in the boot of your car.'

'I'll go and fetch that one then while you sort Mitch out.'

'And I'm afraid there's another in the yard.'

I got Mitch tidied up as best I could, wiped the blood off his face and neck, and bathed his hands. It looked like the fingers on his left hand were broken, but I didn't say anything to him. He was deep in shock. Then I collected up the teeth and put them onto a tissue, just in case they could be saved.

'Milk,' Mitch lisped.

'You want another drink? I'll get you some water.'

'No. Milk – you need to put them in milk. The teeth.'

'Well funnily enough, I haven't got any. Anyway I thought vegans didn't approve of milk.'

He beckoned to me, wanting the teeth. He tucked them inside his cheek.

'Wait,' he mumbled, 'I might have revealed where Abdi lives. Can you…'

'Don't think we need worry about that being passed on. Hush now, Mr Corleone, let's get you out of here.'

I took him outside whilst Taz drove the Peugeot into the unit and came back out again a few minutes later.

'Mikey, take the Jag in there too and perhaps warm it up a little bit to take Sam's prints off.'

'My pleasure, said Mikey.

Me and Mitch sat in the back of the Peugeot and waited. I took his unbroken hand in mine. I looked behind me as Mikey closed the roller shutter doors – inside the orange flames of the burning Jag were casting a glow around the unit.

'Okay, Taz, job done,' said Mikey sitting in the passenger seat.

'Nice one, Mikey.' He turned to me. 'So, Sam. I thought your plan was that we leave you here tied up?'

'You know what? I sort of don't fancy that idea any more.'

'Okay. Let's get out of here before anyone notices.'

He looked into the back seat. 'I think we better get him some medical treatment. We're best heading into London. In the meantime, we can give him something to take the edge off. Mikey – the first aid kit under your seat – there should be some Xanax capsules.'

'We'll probably need somewhere to disappear to for a while as well,' I said.

'We can sort that. And we need to drop this motor off at your mate's garage Mikey. It'll need a respray and new plates now.'

As we turned onto the main road a helicopter flew low overhead.

'That'll be dropping Lord Justice Greedy Bastard off for his round of golf, no doubt,' Taz said.

'No. I know where it's heading,' I threw in idly.

'Oh yeah? Where's that Sam?'

'No, it's nothing.'

'Come on. Spill. Is it linked to that place we've just been to? You mentioned a house earlier.'

'I don't know.'

We neared a junction where Taz pulled over at a turn off.

'Just wait here.' He got out and paced about in front of the car, speaking on his mobile. Mitch sat motionless staring out of the window into an empty field.

Taz then opened the driver door, and as I looked up at him, he took my picture with his phone and shut the door again without speaking. I tried the car door but it was on the child lock. I wound the window down, but Taz wasn't speaking on his phone.

He got back in the driver's seat and turned to look at me, pointing a handgun at me through the gaps in the seats.

'So working undercover are we?'

'That's what I said.'

'We know who you are. So, no more games. Why should I not just kill you now? Pictures of your corpse would be a very good deterrent to add to those of Vernon-Harcourt. You and your fascist mates will have to rethink their strategy then.'

'I've given you what you wanted haven't I? And who was it who killed the driver of the Jag? Do you want to know who that was?'

'Yes, the driver… How did you do that by the way?'

'With a gun, you fuck-wit. He was one of their top intelligence people, he'll be sorely missed: more so than the grunt you took out. Look, can you stop pointing that bloody thing at me?'

'Hand it over then – slowly.'

I couldn't be bothered to argue. I took the gun out and handed it over.

'Nice toy. Okay, tell me about the chopper then, to show me you really have swapped sides.'

'I haven't swapped *sides*. I just care more about this idiot.' Mitch looked at me through half-closed eyes. 'All right. It's probably heading for a house linked to the group.'

'Are you thinking what I'm thinking, Mikey?' said Taz.

'Uh, huh.'

'Sacrificing a few grand's worth of drone for a Jag may not be the best investment, but for a few millions-worth of Agusta helicopter – now that's a decent return on anyone's investment. It will not be quite the same deterrent as a bullet in the head, but perhaps more fun.'

'Right, this is how it is. As a gesture of goodwill, let's call it, you'll take us to somewhere we can park up within half a mile of the place, please.'

Taz turned the car around and we headed towards the house.

'It's the other side of those woods on the right. Get Google Earth up and I'll show you. We pulled off into a farm gateway and I homed in on the satellite view. A bit farther on we turned onto a farm track that headed across some fields.

'Have they got any anti-drone technology, Sam, or Sharon or whoever you are?'

'Let's stick to Sam, shall we? And no, I don't know.'

'Ah well, we'll soon find out. We'll give it a surprise payload, Mikey. Can you land it underneath to take out the fuel tanks?'

'Is the Pope a tosser?'

Taz and Mikey fiddled around in the back for a while. I just couldn't be bothered. Mitch was now asleep with his head on my shoulder. I kept his head leaning forward to stop him swallowing the teeth.

Mikey sat on the passenger seat with the door open playing with his console. He was very quiet. After about five minutes – he let out a little: 'Yes!' He turned to Taz. 'You should have seen that landing, mate. Came in from behind, low and slow, and landed it underneath with barely a bump. Do you want to do the honours?'

'No it's all yours, you've earned it.'

'Bye-bye, little drone, bye-bye helicopter.'

We heard the explosion from the car, and as we drove off a plume of black smoke was rising above the trees into the evening sky.

TWENTY-TWO

I woke up in a rather nice room with the sun coming in in streaks through the curtains. I was in the middle of a double bed looking up at a high ceiling with cut glass chandeliers. The walls were white with some sort of ornate Regency panelling on them. I remembered what had happened. I closed my eyes again, as if by doing so I could make the horror of it go away. Instead the image of the pliers and the blood flashed up across the blank screen. I opened my eyes quickly and focussed on the chandelier above my head: each piece of glass was strung together – was it even a chandelier or just a fancy glass lightshade thing? It was the sort of word everyone used but you probably only really knew the definition of it if you'd got one.

I felt around my mouth with my tongue; there were some gaps at the back but the front teeth were there. I had struggled like hell at first, then must have passed out because – thank God – I couldn't remember. The whole of my mouth was sore: gums, lips tongue. I shuddered. I remembered the weight of my left arm. I had dreamt about it – there was something on it – I lifted it out from under the covers: it was in a pot from the forearm up to my knuckles – just my fingertips poking out.

I eased myself into a sitting position on the side of the bed – my sides were a mass of bruises. I put my weight on my feet – the carpet was real quality. I was wearing pink and white brushed-cotton pyjama bottoms. I went over to the window and parted the curtains to see where I was. I was overlooking a large garden with box hedges arranged in patterns around gravel paths nearest to the house, and lawns beyond.

There was a gentle knock, and the door opened.

'Are you decent?'

'Er, yes. Who is it?'

'I thought I heard movement.' It was a middle-aged, well-spoken woman.

'My name is Mrs Forbes. Doctor Forbes' wife. You're in safe hands. There are some clean clothes on the chair and an en-suite bathroom through that door. Take your time. When you're ready come downstairs and I'll fix you up something to eat.'

'Where am I? How did I get here?'

'In Hampstead, don't worry about anything. Why don't you sort yourself out? Take your time. There'll be plenty of time for questions later.'

I looked in the mirror in the bathroom – my face was bruised and grazed but I didn't look too bad considering. My gums were sore, two teeth at the back were missing and various teeth were wired together, but that was it. There was a walk-in shower with a large fixed showerhead – it was one of the best showers I'd ever had: huge amounts of water and a bottle of posh, orange-flower-scented shower gel. I stayed in for ages feeling the water down my back and my aching sides as I leant against the rail to steady myself and to keep my left arm raised out of the water. The back of my right hand was sore and bruised – it looked like I'd had a cannula in.

I had no recollection of where I was or how I'd got there. I remembered being captive and remembered getting hurt – those bastards that did it to me! But beyond that? Jade? Yes, Jade had been there. She'd looked after me. I was safe. Here felt safe.

There was a huge, white bath-towel and a towelling dressing gown on the back of the door – like in a five star hotel – not that I'd ever been in one.

Back in the room I opened the curtains a bit to let the light in. The clothes that had been put out for me were all new looking – a decent pair of Calvin Klein's, navy blue chinos, socks and Ted Baker shirt. Not quite my thing but they were decent and fitted well.

The wide stairs led down into a large hallway with several rooms leading off. The door to one was open. Mrs Forbes put down her newspaper and came out on seeing me.

'You look much better.'

'I feel better, thanks,' I lisped.

'Come in and sit down, and I'll get you a drink – there's fresh orange and croissants there. You'll probably need to tear them into small pieces – or I could make you some porridge – your mouth will be sore for some time no doubt.'

'My teeth?'

'Don't worry, my husband's friend, Dr Morris, is a dentist – they both worked on you last night. You were a bit of a sight for sore eyes, I'm afraid. Dr Morris thinks your front teeth will be fine.'

'I don't remember anything.'

'You had been sedated and then were given a general anaesthetic. That cocktail, combined with the shock – it's not surprising. Those friends of yours handed your teeth over in a pint of semi-skimmed, so they arrived in good condition. He's left a list of instructions, and some medication, and wants to see you again in a week for follow-up work. You're not to bite or chew anything.'

I tore of a small piece of croissant and sucked it slowly: warm, buttery and definitely not vegan. But, right then, I'd have eaten white veal served with foie gras – well probably not – but I was really hungry.

'Where's Jade?'

'I'm sorry, I don't know who you mean. I saw no girl last night. One of your friends will come round and explain everything. Tea or coffee? Can't let you have it too hot, though.'

'Tea, please. Black.'

'Make yourself at home. There's today's *Guardian* and yesterday's *Observer* if you want to read it. Feel free to wander about the house, but I was told to advise you not to leave the house for now.'

'I feel no urge to go out after what happened.'

'No. I can understand why that might be. But you're young; you'll soon get over it. You can go out into the garden, though, if you like. There's a pair of new shoes for you upstairs too.'

'I'm sorry to put you to all this trouble. Can I pay you for the clothes, at least: once I get sorted out? I've lost everything: phone, wallet, keys.'

'No, don't be silly. We are just glad to be able to do our bit, in our own way, to avert some of the danger this country faces. And we're happy to leave all the chasing around and excitement to young chaps like you.'

'It's not the sort of excitement I'd go looking for. I'm not sure I exactly signed up for this, but thank you, I am very grateful for all you've done for me.'

I flicked through the paper after breakfast; Mrs Forbes left me to myself, saying she would be around if I needed anything. I almost expected what had happened to me to be on the front page – after all, could anything more significant have happened? But then, I suppose, every day in every part of the world, these little dramas take place. Nearly always unnoticed – I suppose we should be grateful for that.

I went back up to my room and found a pair of brown Doc Martens shoes, still in their box. I had always fancied a pair of dockers: but their vegan ones were pricey. Mostly I wore trainers, doubtful though it was that they were more ethical than leather shoes. These dockers were leather: I added them to my growing list of guilty pleasures, along with the croissants.

I wandered round the garden – finding hidden paths, a rose garden and a big tree with a rope swing, no doubt used by grandchildren. I was tempted to give it a go, but thought decorum the better option, especially with a pot on my arm and the state of my ribs.

I found a stone seat next to a small pond and sat and watched water-boatmen flit across the surface. I didn't think I had imagined Jade coming when I was rescued. Perhaps I was wrong to doubt her, perhaps I hadn't been betrayed just when I was at my most vulnerable after all. What had happened? Who had rescued me? Where was she now? Would I see her again? I then remembered that she was on the Fourth Way's hit list – thanks to information I'd given them. I went back to the house and found Mrs Forbes in the kitchen.

'Would home-made vegetable soup be a good idea for lunch?'

'Thank you, that would be nice. I've just been thinking, Mrs Forbes. Someone I care about might be in trouble: she's called Jade, or rather: Kate. Do you know about the Fourth Way or Plan D or whatever they are called? Can I speak to someone about it?'

'I can phone Kenneth, my husband, perhaps. See if he's got his phone switched on.'

'They need to back off her.'

'Leave it with me, Mr Miller.'

'Mitch, is fine.'

'Okay, Mitch. I'll see what I can do. I'll bring lunch through to the dining room for you in a bit.'

I paced about, sat down, paced some more, looked at the pictures in the *Observer* magazine – at the ridiculous outfits costing hundreds of pounds, and restaurant reviews of places in Knightsbridge, places which charged as much for a starter as it would cost to eat out all week at *Make No Bones*. I remembered why I'd stopped buying the *Observer*. I stood up and paced about some more.

Mrs Forbes came in with a tray and placed it on the table.

'Did you manage to get hold of anyone?'

'Yes.'

'And…?'

'I passed your message on.'

'Is that it? No news?'

'I'm sorry Mitch, that's as much as I could do.'

I spent the afternoon dozing on a chaise longue in the window of a room overlooking the garden, in between reading bits of the newspaper and struggling with the puzzles page.

I was woken by the chink of china cups as Mrs Forbes was setting down a tray on the table.

'It's good that you can rest. Here's a fresh pot of tea and some of my famous ginger biscuits. And there's a visitor for you.'

I got up. Abdi was standing in the doorway.

'Come to take you back to Sheffield, mate.'

After Mitch was dropped off somewhere in Hampstead I was blindfolded by a T-shirt being tied round my head, and Mikey sat in the back with me to make sure I didn't sneak a look. We drove for another twenty minutes or so before I was moved to another car and driven for about another twenty. It all seemed a bit stupid to me, but Taz said it was a necessary precaution.

The blindfold was removed after I'd been led into a building.

'So what now?'

'Sleep. We'll decide what to do with you tomorrow – or Monday. No hurry. Do you need the bathroom?'

I nodded. 'I'll fix you up something to eat. Don't try anything funny. All the windows are locked by key and so are the doors, so there's no point trying anything.'

I spent the night with a handcuff attaching my wrist to some bars on the headboard. Not the most comfortable night I'd ever spent but it was preferable to Taz's other suggestion: being handcuffed to him. "It's not my call, sorry," was all he'd say. These people were as mistrusting as the ones on "my side."

I woke up to the Archers theme tune on the radio in the next room and the smell of bacon. A hunt-sab, anarchist-type, listening to the bloody Archers!

I banged on the wall. 'Unlock me or I'll piss in your bed.'

'Morning, girlfriend,' he said opening the door. He was wearing a baggy Clash t-shirt and shorts – presumably what he'd slept in.

'Fuck off,' I replied.

'Yes, it is a beautiful morning and my day has just been lifted beyond description at seeing your beautiful smile.'

He unlocked me. 'You'd better get a shower as well. You stink.'

'Is that surprising? I've not showered since Friday morning or brushed my teeth.'

'You mucky bitch.'

'Very funny. And is there any chance of some clean clothes.'

'I'll see what I can do. I'll ring someone. I don't think any of mine will fit you.'

'No,' I said with as much sarcasm as that word would carry.

The day got better when I sat down after my shower, wrapped in towels, to a fry-up of eggs, bacon, tomatoes, mushrooms and bread.

Some clothes were delivered to the door while I ate. They smelled a bit hippy, like joss sticks or something, and were not a great fit, especially the bra, but were at least clean, after a fashion, though the Che Guevara T-shirt must have been someone's idea of a joke.

'Suits you, that. You know, I could almost start fancying you looking like that.'

'Fuck off. And don't get any funny ideas.'

'What me? I respect women for *who* they are.'

'Yeah, right. Don't you all. Just because you eat tofu, or have some misguided sentimental attachment to rural, ginger vermin, it doesn't mean you're not always on the lookout for an easy shag. Men are men.' His reply was a raised middle finger.

I sat and flicked through Taz's bookshelf that morning while he tapped away on his laptop. He wasn't interested in talking to me and once or twice just showed me his palm as I asked him something, even when I brought him a coffee he just glanced up and nodded, turning the laptop screen away from me so that I couldn't see what he was doing.

The books were mostly boring and worthy left-wing crap by the likes of Gramsci, Tony Benn, and newer stuff by Naomi Klein and that pompous little upstart, Owen Jones. Also one or two incongruous things like an autobiography of Alex Ferguson and a book of Keats' poems.

'What are you going to do with me?'

He looked up, no expression crossed his face, then he went back to his laptop screen.

'Piss off, then.'

I went to the door that led out to the "garden" that qualified it as a garden flat. It was no more than a retaining wall with a patch of overgrown, dandelion-infested grass about three metres by four metres with a washing line draped across it between two ugly, rusting posts. Charming view, imaginative use of space.

'I don't suppose there's any point me asking news of Mitch?'

He didn't even look up this time.

Where did I stand now? Was there any reason why they would keep me alive? It was clear their strategy was to fight back: an eye for an eye, in the hope that the Percies would pull back. There was no way they were going to just let me walk after what I'd done. All's fair in love and war – but somehow I didn't suppose they would see it that way. And what would Mitch be thinking: about what had happened? He was going to blame me for what those goons did to him. But there was no way now that they'd let me see him to even try to explain. The chances were it would end with a bullet in my head and being disposed of somewhere, never to be found.

I went and sat back down in the armchair. I pulled out the Keats and turned the cover page. There was a sticker stuck on which read: "Tanvir Wilder: for achievements in English, St Oswald's school, Year 11." I flicked through and landed on a page where I read the verse:

> *Whene'er the fate of those I hold most dear*
> *Tells to my fearful breast a tale of sorrow,*
> *O bright-eyed Hope, my morbid fancy cheer;*
> *Let me awhile thy sweetest comfort borrow:*
> *Thy heaven-born radiance around me shed,*
> *And wave thy silver pinions o'er my head.*

I was also particularly taken by a preface to a poem he wrote when he was just twenty-two: where he is full of doubt about himself and his future – a period in between boyhood and manhood when his "soul is in torment, the character undescribed, the way of life uncertain." How true that felt right then.

What would I do if my life were to be spared? It was clear that Fate's cog had clunked forward on the ratchet, that something had changed within me, that my priorities had changed – my whole character undecided. If I could have just one thing right now… Oh, of course, even then it might never work out. Lord knows there would be enough barriers to negotiate, and reasons why not, but:

> *O let me think it is not quite in vain,*
> *To sigh out sonnets to the midnight air.*

I read on until towards midday, Taz blindfolded me again and led me outside.

'Where are we going?'

'For a debrief, and to decide what to do with you.'

'Can't you just let me go?'

'After what you've done? No chance. There needs to be some sort of process.'

'Like a kangaroo court or something?'

'No, not like that – but a rational decision based on evidence.'

'An interrogation?'

'A structured, cognitive interview, let's say. Also we can't let you go back to doing what you were doing before can we?'

'I won't. I've had enough. Couldn't I just disappear somewhere. Go off to South America or something? Take Mitch with me. I just want to see him again. Where is he?'

'He's being looked after.' There was a pause. 'What if we were to let it be known how you helped us?'

'You wouldn't... You bastard.'

'You must admit it would solve the problem of how we were going to kill you. We'd just let your friends do it.'

'What is it you want out of this? For them to back off, right? For at least a stalemate to be declared? Well there is another way. You potentially hold an ace in your hand.'

'Just save it, yeah? I don't want to hear it.'

I heard a black cab pull up. Taz led me out by the arm, his big clumsy hand encircling my bicep in his grip, and sat me in.

'I'm taking her to a surprise party, mate – it's her birthday.' He squeezed my arm tight. 'The address is on that piece of paper. Mum's the word, eh?'

'Right you are.'

TWENTY-FOUR

The police initially tried to keep the kidnapping of the daughter of John Fitzwilliam-Bryce a secret.

At first they thought it was just somebody trying to blackmail one of Britain's wealthiest families into parting with a lot of money. They deployed the usual tactics of trying to control all communications to and from the kidnappers: trying to play for time to work out the location to arrange for a handover that would lead the perpetrators into a trap, or at least unwittingly giving away intelligence.

They put all this in place and awaited further contact from the kidnappers, beyond the initial letter from his daughter. But it did not go according to plan at all. The story somehow leaked out on to social media. This made no sense – if you were wanting a ransom why jeopardize that by letting the story go public? Unless it was the family that leaked it; but they had been told not to risk provoking the kidnappers into doing something stupid, and they understood that – it couldn't have been them.

Then no demands for money were forthcoming, and there was no group claiming responsibility: so it didn't appear to be a blackmailer, a terrorist, or someone wanting publicity.

After a few months the whole story went quiet, and it was over dinner at the House of Lords that a discussion took place between a representative of the family, a cabinet minister and a senior official with strong links to the security services. It was made clear that the case was to be closed.

*

The General Election campaign was being fought in a way that most people thought was refreshing. The bitterness and backstabbing that had characterised previous elections and the Referendum was missing. The competing parties put their differing messages strongly, but with some regard to avoiding whipping up hatred – almost as if they had come to the edge of a cliff and decided to pull back. Even things like evidence and facts re-emerged.

Those at the extremes on either side had not continued to gain momentum in the ways it once looked they might. Some put this down to the public recoiling in horror from what it saw politicians trying to do with *their* votes – there was a genuine desire amongst the majority for a kinder, more honest kind of politics.

Brutal murders on both sides had ripped the old political fabric. To spout vitriol and hatred became a vote loser, or led to a haemorrhaging of readers.

TWENTY-FIVE

A good-looking woman sat in her first class seat at St Pancras International waiting for the train for Brussels to depart. She had red hair, cropped in a pageboy style under a knitted beret. She wore a tight-fitting, pencil skirt and neat little leather jacket.

Another woman, middle-aged and equally stylish in her own way approached, looking for her own seat, and sat down opposite her. She smiled at the young woman and took a half bottle of champagne from her bag.

'I'm celebrating my divorce and a new start. I have a spare plastic cup if you've anything to celebrate?'

The young woman smiled. 'A new start for me too. So, I don't mind if I do, thank you.'

'So, what is it, a new job?'

'Sort of. But also freedom after quite some time where I was not able to come and go as I chose.'

'A controlling relationship? That sounds so familiar.'

'Sort of. It's complicated – I can't go into it. But now I'm going to meet my boyfriend, who I've not seen for well over a year. We've only been able to communicate through letters. Lots of letters. He's in Brussels.'

'Oh that's lovely. So exciting. So romantic. I'll drink to that!'

They both raised their plastic glasses.

'To a new start!'

The train glided north then dipped and curved into the tunnel.

'So, does he work out there?'

'Yes. In a little restaurant that specialises in vegetarian and vegan food.'

Acknowledgements

Those closest to me for putting up with this daft writing thing I've become obsessed with: especially Helen for reading all the rubbish I keep churning out. Simon for support and incisive comments, and showing me some of the sights of Tottenham. Elaine for reading the draft and for equally useful comments.

1889 Books

My website www.1889books.co.uk contains information on my other books.

The Evergreen in red and white is a novel about the first Romani gypsy to play for England: Rab Howell. Set in Sheffield in 1897-98, it follows Rab through his last turbulent year in the city as he struggles to do the right thing having fallen in love with another woman.

I have also published three other forgotten classics: *The Skipper's Wooing* by W W Jacobs, *Spirit of Old Essex*, a collection of works by Arthur Morrison, and *Put Yourself in his Place* by Charles Reade.

The Bantams of Sheffield is Sheffield's second oldest novel and the first novel to feature the local dialect.

Historical Football Stories is a collection of the oldest football (soccer) stories in the world.

Joe Stepped off the Train is a collection of short stories by a diverse group of authors from which all author royalties go to the charity *War Child*.

Seditious Things: The Songs of Joseph Mather – Sheffield's Georgian Punk Poet is out in the summer of 2017 as is *How Great a Crime – to speak the truth*. Both are non-fiction and between them tell of an important chapter in Sheffield's history.

Thanks.

You can get in touch via facebook.com/SteveK1889, Twitter.com/SteveK1889 or e-mail me at stevek1889@gmail.com